DEATH OF A TANGO KING

DEATH
OF A

TANGO

KING

JEROME CHARYN

NEW YORK UNIVERSITY PRESS
New York and London

NEW YORK UNIVERSITY PRESS
New York and London

Library of Congress Cataloging-in-Publication Data
Charyn, Jerome.
Death of a tango king / Jerome Charyn.
p.   cm.
ISBN 0-8147-1575-3 (acid-free paper)
I. Title.
PS3553.H33D43   1998
813′.54—dc21   97-33913
                                CIP

New York University Press books are printed on acid-free paper,
and their binding materials are chosen for strength and durability.

Manufactured in the United States of America

10 9 8 7 6 5 4 3 2 1

For Paco Taibo

YOLANDA

1

THE LESBIANS wouldn't leave her alone. They scribbled notes to Yolanda. They smuggled chocolate bars into her cell. They invited her to the big dance. They called themselves the Hell Sisters, and the entire prison ran to their particular clock. There would have been no mashed potatoes in the mess hall, no Wednesday night film, no art classes or poetry meetings, without these Sisters. The warden shivered around them, because they seemed to have connections in terribly high places. They got letters from state senators, poetry societies, and the governor himself. And Warden Kaplan only had three more years to go until retirement. She didn't want to risk the animus of the Sisters. So she let them have their way.

And Yolanda suffered because of this. Their leader was Marcelline O'Roarke, a published poet who liked to forge checks. Marcelline was a French-Irish-puertorriqueña who ran the prison farm with all the fury of her intelligence and her wit. She was a head shorter than Yolanda, and her cropped hair made her look like a fuzzy egg with eyelashes.

"I'm in love with you, Yolanda . . . I want you to be my wife. You can live with me and go to all my poetry readings. We'll be rich."

"I have a son, Marcelline. He's five."

"Yes, I know. The warden lets me read all the files. His name is Benjamin. And he's staying in a foster home while you're in the can. I can give him an allowance, Yolanda. I can get him into a good school. I have the pull. Trust me."

"But I'm in love with a man," Yolanda said. "He's doing time in Green Haven."

"Forget about him," Marcelline said. "He'll never make it."

All the men she'd ever had were jailbirds. Yolanda's current fiancé had taught her the art of robbing banks. She wasn't in love with him. That was a lie. But she didn't want Marcelline to think she was some stray chicken who could be pressed into service, become a concubine of the Hell Sisters. Marcelline had terrific biceps under the Hawaiian shirt she wore at Harrington Hills, but Yolanda didn't have a fascination for women's biceps. If she had to live all her life in a world without men, she might have chosen a chicita who was tall and slim, not a muscle-bound poet who bragged a lot.

Besides, Yolanda was in love with the college professor who flew in from Cornell once a week to offer a philosophy course to the women at Harrington Hills. The professor was a volunteer in the prison outreach program. He wasn't paid a dime. Yet he had the devotion of a young priest. He would wear his galoshes to class. His shirt was torn at the elbow. He had a squint in one eye. He was into ecology and all that Save the Planet shit.

"There's no more air to breathe," the professor said. His name was Sparks, Melvin P. He had holes in his pants. "The planet's been fouling itself. Our forests are dying, ladies. Do you know what that dying is called?"

"Yeah, yeah," Yolanda said. "The big bald greenhouse. It's a nasty mother. It eats up air and everything. Because a big bald house can't absorb carbon monoxide and all the other lousy gasses. And with all the uneaten carbon monoxide, the earth starts to warm up. Those lousy gasses are lying over our heads, waiting to piss on our future."

"But our future, Yolanda, is an ecological time bomb. We're all little Cassandras, prophetesses no one will believe. So we die and die and die . . ."

"That's your opinion," said Marcelline, looking at Yolanda and the prof. "I'd say there's a lot of greenhouse gasses right in this room. And that gas is Melvin P. Sparks, who isn't even certified to teach in this jail. I can play Cassandra, like anybody else. Mr. Sparks, what department are you with up at Cornell? The poetry department? The ecology department? Because I can't seem to find your name in the catalogue."

"I float around a lot . . . from project to project."

"Ah," Marcelline said, "the floating prof. Well, you'd better float right out of here, before I write a letter to the warden. And then we'll see who is qualified to teach. I like my Cornell profs to come from Cornell."

Sparks packed his belongings. And Yolanda was mortified. Because his lectures were the only high point she had. She would have slid into a terrible gloom without Professor Sparks. She didn't like that constant serenading of Marcelline O'Roarke. She didn't like the extra chocolate from the Hell Sisters, because it was the same as a poisoned kiss. She wanted to do her time and get back to little Benjamin, or else she'd always be a stranger to her son.

The lesbians wouldn't leave her alone. Marcelline's lieutenant, Big Nell, bumped against her in the shower room. "You hurt Marcy's feelings, you little bitch." Nell had copious hair on her forearms. She was the hairiest person Yolanda had ever seen.

"I'm practically engaged, Nell. I couldn't cheat on my man."

"Engagements don't count in the can. Forget your other life, girl. Marcy's taken pity on you. Or we would have swiped your cherry months ago. You'll be paddling in a river of blood if you can't get your priorities straight. Now don't you disrespect me, girl."

"I wouldn't dis you, Nell," Yolanda said.

"Then swear you'll marry Marcelline."

Nell was holding a plank with a nail sticking out, like some kind of crazy hammer that could peck away at Yolanda's skull. Nell had crowned other reluctant brides with the hammer. And Yolanda couldn't run to the warden, because wardens didn't mean much at the farm. Harrington Hills had become a country club for the Hell Sisters. And Yolanda was one more piece of pie.

"I swear," she said.

Yolanda had grown up in the barrio. Her pappy had died before she was ten. Her people were from Colombia, but she'd never been outside the barrio until she arrived at Harrington Hills. Colombia was the land of cocaine and emeralds, but Yolanda had gone to jail because the man she loved was a bank robber, and bank robbers had become a lost romantic tribe in Nueva York. The policía could appear at any bank in ninety seconds, and that wasn't enough margin for even the best bank robber. And her fiancé had to pick on Chase Manhattan Bank, which had its own policía. Yolanda wasn't even holding a gun.

"I'm lonely," her man had said. "Yolanda, come with me."

And like a fool she'd followed him to the bank, which was right on Broadway, and had more alarms than a city of firetrucks. Her fiancé had promised that she would only have to leave little Benjamin for fifteen minutes, no mas. And that fifteen minutes turned into two years. She entered the bank with a blush on her face, dreaming of a new father for Benjamin . . . and enough money to open a pequeño candy store on the corner of Madison and a Hundred and Twenty-ninth, where the old chocolate factory used to be. Yolanda would clean out the cucarachas and the rats. But the policía fell on Yolanda outside Chase Manhattan Bank. The court gave her an abogado who tried to get into her pants. Yolanda bit him on the hand. She lived at Rikers Island, among all the cucarachas and the rats. A new abogado presented himself. His name was Don Alfredo. He wore dark boots and a shirt made of silk. He looked at her titas. Yolanda didn't like him.

"Tell the court I don't want their abogados."

"I'm not from the court, sweet Yolanda. I'm a gift from your little cousin, Ruben Falcone."

"I don't remember such a cousin, señor."

"Ah, you used to call him Ruben the Squirrel. You played doctor with him behind your mother's sink."

"He was a squirrel because he touched me in all the wrong places . . . but who told you about the sink?"

"Ruben did. He wants to help you. He heard about your tragedy."

"I haven't seen him in twenty years. Where is the little bastard."

"In Medellín, Dona Yolanda. He's a famous man."

"If he's so famous, Don Alfredo, why doesn't he come himself? He should pay respects to his own cousin."

"Ah, he is not free to do so."

"You mean, he's one of the Medellín crowd. A coca man, the king of the cartel."

"Something like that. He cannot advertise his position. But he would not forget a cousin like you."

But this abogado, the friend of Ruben Falcone, was as antsy as the other. He would sing love songs through the wire window at the women's house of detention where Yolanda sat, because she had no bail bondsman to deliver her.

"I want to see my son, I want to see my son," she told the abogado. And Don Alfredo started to fidget.

"If you were to become rich all of a sudden, it would reveal our hand. So you will have to stay in this pig's house a little longer."

And that's when Yolanda began to have premonitions that this abogado wasn't as close to Ruben as he liked to think. He was trying to profit on Ruben's name. He was pitiful in court. The prosecutor and the judge took their turns bullying Don Alfredo, and they buried Yolanda, painting her as the merciless mama of Madison and a Hundred and Twenty-ninth. She got five to nine for armed robbery, and she'd never been near a gun.

The lesbians wouldn't leave her alone. First at the courthouse, then at Rikers, and now at Harrington Hills. Yolanda wasn't afraid of Big Nell, but if she didn't become Marcelline's puta, she'd have a couple of holes in her head, and she might never see her baby again.

"The consecration will be tomorrow night," Nell told her, and Yolanda almost started to laugh. Because the Hell Sisters had all these little rituals. They would dress up Yolanda as a bride, with a veil and a long white dress, one of them would play the priest, and they'd offer Yolanda to Marcelline, right in the prison chapel. And she couldn't go and complain to Warden Kaplan, because the warden was so bamboozled by the Hell Sisters, she'd give her blessing to the marriage.

Yolanda had never been married before. She'd had plenty of fiancés, but the barrio was short of bridegrooms. She'd have a jailhouse wedding, with the Hell Sisters as groomsmen and bridesmaids. The bridegroom herself was a poet with spectacular biceps. Yolanda could have done worse. She'd never had much luck with men. But she just couldn't imagine kissing a fuzzy egg with eyelashes, like Marcelline O'Roarke.

She stayed in her cell long before evening call. She didn't have the heart to face her future bridegroom. The Sisters would have gloated at her and tried to fit Yolanda with her wedding veil. The whole bridal shop would have to work full steam, or they couldn't produce Yolanda's dress. She didn't bother to sleep. She thought about Professor Sparks. She didn't care if he wasn't from Cornell. What was Cornell to her? A mating ground for rich girls. Yolanda couldn't even graduate from high school.

She waited at her window for dawn to come. It was the quietest time at Harrington Hills. The night owls would shut off their radios after four. The gamblers would give up their cards. The sleepwalkers would fall asleep. The screws would stop patrolling the cell blocks. And Yolanda would have all that silence to herself. She could feel the world. It was palpable at five in the morning, because the chicas at Harrington Hills weren't moving around and breathing so much. Yolanda could suck in the night air. She watched for the first fuzzy line of light in the blue-black sky. Only the sky wasn't black. It was more like a bottomless green. Sparks had told her what that was all about. The greenhouse gasses were eating up all the atmosphere. The curtain of ozone that shielded Yolanda from the sun was beginning to crack. And the dawn looked like a soft copper dome filled with octopus ink. The day began with little squirts of poisoned copper ink. It seemed like a good omen for a marriage.

2

THE CHICAS stared at her during breakfast. Yolanda couldn't finish her bran muffin. The prison seamstress visited her table. The seamstress's name was Jim. She told Yolanda that her fitting would be at half past ten. "Don't be late. Marcy wouldn't like it."

Then one of the screws came up to Yolanda. "Kaplan wants to see you, girl. Right away."

Yolanda was led out of the mess hall, across the cell blocks, through the big iron door, and up to the warden's office, which wasn't much bigger than Yolanda's crib. It didn't seem worth it to have a warden's chair if that was all the reward you got. But then Yolanda remembered that Kaplan could graduate from Harrington Hills every day of the week. She was doing salaried time. The state was giving her dollars to sit in that chair. Yolanda had all the arrogance of a jailhouse mama.

Kaplan was close to sixty. She didn't have mean eyes.

"I hear you're getting married."

"Mrs. Kaplan, I'd like to make it to my next birthday. I have a son. I want to see him."

"I could put you in isolation."

"So I'd be a bachelor woman for another month. The Sisters will find me. I might as well marry the girl."

"I don't have to tell you about Marcelline. She likes long courtships and very short marriages. She'll farm you out to the other Sisters."

"Mrs. Kaplan, I won't last much longer if I don't wear the veil. Being married makes me a Hell Sister. And I might have a chance from the inside. I don't have much of a chance right now."

"But you do, my dear," the warden said. And Yolanda didn't like that 'my dear.' She was a convict, a bank robber (without a gun), and not some chica in a nursery school.

"A man wants to see you . . . he's come all the way from Q Street in the capital. He's one of the Christian Commandos."

"What Christian Commandos? You mean, those environmental cowboys who love to dive into forest fires? I read about them in a comic book. They have their own priesthood and everything. They don't drink or smoke or mingle with women . . . this Christian Commando looking for a concubine?"

"Shhh," the warden said. "Don't be disrespectful, my dear. Will you see him or not?"

"Sure I'll see him. But I'd rather marry Marcelline than be a Christian Commando's wife. I ain't so fond of eunuchs."

"Yolanda, watch your tongue."

Mrs. Kaplan escorted Yolanda into another room and

then excused herself. There was a man in the room with his back toward Yolanda. He wasn't wearing a uniform, because the Commandos didn't have one. They were civilians soldiers—cowboys and cops. He turned and faced Yolanda. His hair was slicked down, like some Valentino. He wore a white shirt and a dark tie that was knotted at the neck. He wore a blue suit. His nails were clean. He didn't have any holes in his pants.

Yolanda had never been so disappointed in a man.

"I liked you better, Mr. Whoever-you-are, when you were a simple prof from Cornell. I don't have much use for environmental dicks."

He laughed at Yolanda. He had his old, goofy smile.

"What is your name, anyhow?"

"Melvin P. Sparks. I'm sorry about the masquerade. But we had to be cautious."

"Cautious about what?"

"Recruiting you for the environmental rangers."

"Oh, is that what you call yourselves. I thought you were the Christian Commandos."

"Yolanda, we aren't soldiers. We inhabit a no-man's-land, somewhere between yesterday's peace and tomorrow's war."

"Since when do you take convicts into your cadre?"

"Whenever we need them. We aren't civil servants, not in the strictest sense. We can hire and fire as we please. Your name would never be on any of our books. You'd be paid in cash . . . and you aren't subject to any income taxes."

"That's the Commandos, all right. And I suppose you want me for my looks."

He laughed again. And it hurt Yolanda to think how much handsomer he was in his teaching rags.

"Yes, your looks, Yolanda. And your proximity to Ruben Falcone."

"Now I get it," she said, her eyes a fierce green, like the emeralds of the Andes and the Amazon. "You want me to become your snitch. Call yourself whatever you like. You're nothing but a fancy spook. And I'm not joining your army."

"Yolanda, I wouldn't hurt your cousin, even if he is a coca man. But he's hiding out in the jungle, and half a dozen agencies are hoping to fry his ass. Meanwhile, they're destroying the rain forest around Ruben. We can't afford that loss of acreage. To hell with all those high-profile drug cops. They can't catch the little king. And if the war against Ruben goes on much longer, we'll have a rain forest that's fucking bald."

"And all the greenhouse gasses," Yolanda said. "I listened to your rap, Professor Sparks. I believed in you."

"You're the best student I ever had."

"Do you visit a lot of women's penitentiaries, Professor?"

"No, it's my first time out."

"Then why couldn't you knock on my door. I'm not hard to find. I have my own crib in Cell Block Five."

"You wouldn't have talked to a stranger."

"You are a stranger. You're worse than that. You're a snake. You fool a girl, you give her high expectations, and then you bite her on the ass with your own brand of poison."

"Yolanda, they'll kill him. He doesn't have a prayer. Help us set up a dialogue. He'll trust you. You were babies together. I don't want Ruben. I want him out of the rain forest."

"Should I tell him I'm with the CIA, the FBI, the federales, and the secret police? No thank you. He's better off where he is."

"Just train with us. I'll get you out of the can. Then you can decide for yourself."

She thought of the wedding that was waiting for her, her bondage to the Hell Sisters. "I'll think it over."

"Damn you. You don't have time to think."

She considered the veil she'd have to wear, and Marcelline's spit all over her body. "I want to see my little boy."

"We're not guidance counselors. I have a program to run. It's already off schedule."

"Give me Baby Benjamin, or I don't move from this can."

"Impossible," the professor said. But his voice began to break.

"One hour, jefe, one hour with my little boy. And then I'm yours."

❧

She was whisked out of Harrington Hills. She never even returned to her crib. The seamstress would have to catch Yolanda in another life. Sparks had a wardrobe waiting for her. There were no wedding dresses. People must have told Sparks all of Yolanda's "vital signs," because the shoes and socks and shirts didn't come out of any Salvation Army cellar. They had a Manhattan label. And Yolanda wasn't so sure she liked having Sparks pick her underpants. Him and his Christian Commandos.

She was in a black limo with Venetian blinds. Sparks smoked cigarillos on the journey down from Harrington Hills. The chauffeur sat behind a glass wall. Yolanda couldn't see more than his barest outline. Sparks conversed with him though a little phone that was built into the leather. The blinds were shut, and Yolanda couldn't even tell when they'd arrived in the barrio. The limo stopped. Sparks opened the door. Yolanda recognized the craters of a Hundred and Twenty-ninth Street. Then a figure stood in front of her. A little man in boy's clothes. Yolanda started to cry. She recognized the hombre who had once been her baby boy. He was six or seven. Yolanda must have lost a couple of years while she was in the can.

She turned to Sparks. "Jesus, Professor, can't you give me a little privacy?"

"Miz Yolanda, we don't have the time."

"You'll give the boy the wrong impression . . . he'll think you're my husband or something like that."

"Then I'll introduce myself." He reached across Yolanda and squeezed the boy's hand. "How are you, Ben?"

The boy had dark hair and his mama's green eyes. His face was almost too beautiful for a boy. He looked like some cherub who'd walked out of a Manhattan ruin. He wore mittens, a scarf, and a long leather coat.

"I'm your mother's employer, Ben. She kinda works for me."

Yolanda couldn't stop crying. "If you don't get out of the car, Professor Sparks, I'll piss all over the seats and eat all the upholstery."

"Wouldn't do that, Yolanda. It's on loan from the Justice Department. I'd have a hard time explaining the damage . . . technically I'm not entitled to a car."

He slipped past Yolanda and out the door. And Yolanda

invited the little man up into the cushions beside her. The boy seemed hesitant. Then he started to climb.

"Yolanda," he said, as if she'd just stepped out of the house to rob that bank and had only been gone two hours. "Did you decide to be someone else's mama?"

"No, Benjamin. The bad people took your mammy away."

He climbed closer until he was near Yolanda's face.

"Then I forgive you, mama."

And Yolanda realized that she'd do anything—scratch, kill, betray a cousin, rob another bank—to get Benjamin back.

THE MAN FROM Q STREET

3

H E C O U L D N ' T requisition a train ticket, so he had
to drive her to D.C. in the big car that should have been in
the garage at Justice. The Christian Commandos didn't even
have a proper bank account. Sparks had to make bookings
with his own blood. He borrowed and stole. And when there
was a sudden spillover of cash, Sparks had to spend and
spend to keep his little ship afloat. His one solitary unit
existed in the cracks between Justice, Defense, and State. It
should have been attached to the Environmental Protection
Agency, but the director, Mrs. Fannie Morrison, wouldn't
tolerate a maverick group of policemen in her "dossier." She
was hoping to make a run for the vice-presidency in '96, and
she couldn't afford a gang of Keystone Kops who might
bring her bad publicity. Fannie's motto was "Safe causes for
a safer time." And that didn't include clandestinos mucking
around in the Orinoco River basin. "Let another agency
take the heat. This is America. I don't need monkey business
in Venezuela or Peru."

And so, officially, Sparks was on a fact-finding mission for the EPA. He worked for Mrs. Fannie. He'd been a Defense Department analyst until he was drummed out of the service during the "Kristallnacht" of '92, when heretics like him were let go. Earlier he'd been with State. He was Bruno West's wonderboy. The brilliant undersecretary of state for East Asian affairs had been educated at Harvard, Princeton, and Yale. He was a member of the Triangle Club and all that crap. And Sparks had gone to a little Baptist college in the Bible Belt. He was the son of an embezzler. His daddy had died in a West Texas jail. But he got along with Bruno. They both had the misfortune of being a little too *un*American. They wouldn't manufacture enemies, like State often did. Bruno wanted to institute a Marshall Plan for North Vietnam. He wanted to rebuild the rain forests. He got a note from the president. "Mr. Undersecretary, if you'd like to lobby for the gooks, do it on your own fucking time." Bruno wouldn't argue. He returned to his farm in Vermont. He was fifty-two at the time. He had his own modest fortune. He prospered, but he couldn't seem to stay put. And so he started the Christian Commandos. First with his fortune, and then finagling here and there. He ran a "research company" that had one client: the United States. His field chief was Melvin P. Sparks, who was on loan from that public nuisance, Mrs. Fannie Morrison. Sparks could have gone to jail, like his dad, if he didn't have some kind of quasi-governmental status. Mrs. Fannie was their favorite umbrella.

But they had a hard time moving funds around. They could only hire independent contractors, like Yolanda, who wouldn't surface on someone else's payroll. It was a constant fight for cash. They had to train an army, shelter it, move it from spot to spot, without any formal appropriation. Bruno danced a lot with different partners. Justice, Defense, Treasury, State, Interior, the White House itself. His "research teams" were tolerated, but no one wanted to give them a home.

They had a house on Q Street, headquarters of the Phalanx Project. The only visible employees were Mrs. Anita Frame, a secretary borrowed from Justice, and Sparks himself, who lived there in a closet at the back of the house. He didn't draw a salary. There was nothing to draw. And he couldn't park Yolanda on Q Street, because someone might have noticed. So he had her double up with Mrs. Anita in her Georgetown flat until she could start her basic training at the Commandos' boot camp, a makeshift farm in tidewater country. The drill instructors were retired marines who liked the romance of environmental soldiers . . . and the feel of hard currency in their pockets.

Sparks only had a couple of dollars to give Yolanda. He kissed her on the forehead outside Mrs. Anita's flat.

"Promise me, Professor, I won't lose my son."

"Miz Yolanda, I will go into Family Court and destroy the fucking place if I have to."

"And I won't go back to jail?"

"Not while Melvin P. Sparks is still alive."

Sparks rode to Q Street and dismissed his driver, who would sneak the limo back into Justice's motor pool. Sparks had completed one more phantom trip, from D.C. to Harrington Hills and home again. Bruno had arranged Yolanda's invisible "parole" through Justice. It took six months. Each day Yolanda spent with the Commandos would be considered two days of jail time. New York's Department of

Corrections was happy to get rid of Yolanda. Whatever trouble she caused would be part of Justice's show. Bruno West had to hock his own life before Justice would intercede for him. The Phalanx Project and all its assets, visible and invisible, extant or not, were now property of the Justice Department. Sparks didn't care. He had his girl.

He was surprised to find a light on in Bruno's office. He wondered if it was a burglar. Half a dozen other agencies were always tapping into Bruno's files, sometimes with permission, sometimes not. Sparks stepped lightly into the house. He had a goddamn pistol, with a permit from the Justice Department, but he didn't like to wear it. It created bulges under his heart. Sparks was proud of his trim lines. He was field chief of the Phalanx Project. He had to present an image for the agents he ran, even if his most reliable agent was Sparks.

He climbed the stairs. He made a bit of noise. If there was a lad in Bruno's office, Sparks wanted to give him enough time to hop onto the roof. He sang the Commandos' little anthem.

> We are the Christian Commandos
> We fight for Mother Earth
> From dawn to dusk we go
> From dusk to dawn . . .

He knocked on Bruno's door. He entered the office. The light had been switched off. Someone sat in the dark, near Bruno's attic window.

"Sonny boy," Sparks said. "Take what you're looking for and get the hell out."

The figure didn't move. Then Sparks heard the familiar

suck of a cigarette lighter. It was his boss, director of the Phalanx Project.

"Christ, Bruno, why are you sitting in the dark?"

The lamp went on. Bruno was holding a gun aimed at Sparks' groin. He had white, white hair. He was sixty-nine. He had the profile of a movie star. He could have run Xerox or Remington Rand. He had all the right credentials. But he preferred the insane vocabulary and accouterments of the Christian Commandos.

"Sparks, don't come up on a man like that, humming our battle songs . . . I thought it was a spook from the White House."

"Mind pointing that gun in a different direction? I don't want to lose my pecker . . . and why would the White House be so interested in us?"

"Because we're going to ruin their favorite project, the capture and evisceration of Ruben Falcone, numero uno drug merchant and king of the Medellín cartel."

Bruno still had his gun on Sparks' groin, as if he couldn't make up his mind about the authenticity of his own field chief.

"Bruno, the president is sponsoring us. He contributes to our kitty. Why would he want to raid our files?"

"Because he's a son of a bitch. He likes to humor me. He thinks we'll never get King Ruben, but he isn't sure. If the Drug Enforcement people find out that the White House is contributing to our ops, the shit will fly all over the place. And now that you've captured Ruben's little cousin, we might have a chance. She is in your custody, Sparks, or am I wrong?"

"Staying with Mrs. Anita until we ship her to the farm."

In one long, lazy motion, Bruno let the gun fall into his pocket. "Unguarded?"

"Christ, Anita's one of us. If I suspected any trouble, I'd have whisked her out of Washington."

"Is she a clever girl?"

"Clever enough."

"But will she give us trouble, Sparks?"

"Not while her boy is in custody of the courts."

"We don't want to blackmail her, Sparks. I'm against that."

"Then call it indoctrination . . . we aren't going to kill Ruben, are we, sir?"

"Wouldn't consider it," Bruno said. "We're not cannibals, you know. We don't swallow our own kind."

"But are we going to kill him, sir?"

"Not if we can help it. But we might not be able to control the scenario, son . . ."

"Meaning what?"

"Well, for one thing, it depends on how many agencies are in the picture."

"But we'll get to him first. That's the whole point of the expedition."

"Indeed, but we'll have to let the other lads interrogate him . . . even if only for a little while. They have paid for the privilege, you know. We can't get on some high horse. We have to be practical, Sparks, or Phalanx could disappear overnight."

"But I promised her that the little king wouldn't be touched."

"And we'll do our best to keep that promise . . . I'm not a butcher, Sparks. I won't sell Ruben to the DEA, if that's what you mean. Now get some rest."

He departed with his briefcase, this patrician knight of the rain forests. He mingled with senators, discovered secret sources of cash, made alliances that Sparks would have to honor. There wouldn't have been any Christian Commandos without Bruno West. Sparks didn't have the vision or the fortitude or the connections to create the Commandos. He couldn't thrust his image upon the planet the way Bruno could. He was a simple chief with his own boot camp. An embezzler's boy. He trudged downstairs, drank a glass of milk, and went up to his closet.

4

FIVE MINUTES into that rotten camp and Yolanda knew it was going to be a big mistake. Mosquitoes socked at her eyes. She saw a snake. And this farm that belonged to the Christian soldiers was as much of a prison as Harrington Hills. It was worse than having cell blocks. Her barrack-bungalow swam around in six inches of mud. "It's the tide-water," Yolanda's drill instructor said. "Means nothing, girl."

Yolanda trained in mud. She slept in mud. She had mud between her toes. She tasted mud in the mess hall. She looked at mud in the latrine. "That's jungle conditions, girl. We're simulatin' the Magdalena Valley for you. You're our Amazon mud baby, our Orinoco shock sister."

It was kind of sad training all alone, without the company of other people. Yolanda had become her own platoon. She and the drill instructor, whose name was Harve, were the last two inhabitants of a hundred and twenty acres of swamp. Harve was only human. He wanted to get into her pants.

"I could fall for you, Yolanda, real hard."

"Sir, I'm sorry, sir," she said, trying to keep to the language of a recruit. "But this rookie is engaged to a bank robber, sir. The bank robber's doing some hard time. And I couldn't dream of being unfaithful, sir . . . not with my own D.I."

Harve turned a little mean. He must have figured that he'd have Yolanda all to himself in this little kindergarten of the Christian Commandos, called Snakepit Farms. He was sixty, and he hadn't done much soldiering since Nam. Sparks had recruited him out of an A.A. meeting in the cellar of a Baptist church.

"You ain't a rookie," Harve said. "You're a piece of shit. Now give me fifty."

Yolanda had to get down in the mud and do fifty pushups for her demented D.I. The man's gonna kill me, the man's gonna kill me, she kept muttering to herself.

But Harve grew quiet after he had a swallow of wine. "It's alcohol," he said, with a glaze in his eye. "I just can't get rid of the bottle, girl."

And he looked so desperate, so full of loathing for himself, that Yolanda took him in her arms, rocked him like an enormous baby. She didn't think it was the right protocol, but things were already peculiar at this pestilential place. Yolanda stopped caring. And it was only then that Harve showed her what kind of drill instructor he could be. He took her through every single obstacle at Snakepit Farms. He taught her how to shoot a gun, to survive in a jungle on a lick of purified water and salt, to wrap her shins in cotton so she wouldn't bang them in the brush and develop horrible sores. She climbed monkey ladders, lived in the swamp, learned how to kill a man with one tap on the temples, though it bothered her that environmental cowboys would want to make an assassin out of Yolanda. She could start a fire in the wettest climate, feed herself on bark and bitter berries, wash herself in black mud.

And just when she was beginning to appreciate boot camp with Harve, the professor arrived with a little gang of people. Sparks stood in the background. There was a new professor now. He didn't seem to have much use for Yolanda. He scorned her training at the farm. He smiled like a handsome rat with yellow teeth. His fingers smelled of tobacco. His gums were a little green. He didn't wear khaki like the others did. He wore a charcoal-colored suit in the Commandos' simulated jungle. Yolanda knew there was no way she could flatter this man.

"General," she said, figuring he was the leader of the whole shebang. "General, did I do good?"

"I'm not a general," he told her. "Did you catch any stars on my shoulder? We're civilians here . . . you can call me Bruno."

"Well, Mr. Bruno, did I pass basic training?"

"Your training hasn't started yet. You've been on a picnic."

"But I'm a marksman now."

He laughed, and he had dirty little eyes under all that handsomeness. "Daughter, you won't need a gun. Do you know how much you've cost us so far? We had to bribe half a prison."

"Sir," she said, "that isn't my fault."

"We're sending you to Medellín, the murder capital of the world. It makes Beirut look like a carnival . . . corpses rot in the street. The electricity is very fickle. And you have to pay with your life for a glass of water. Do you think you're up to that?"

"Have you ever lived on Madison and a Hundred and Twenty-ninth? We do our own electricity. I'm not worried, Mr. Bruno."

Bruno West clapped his hands and winked at Sparks. "I'm beginning to like our little daughter. I believe she'll do, Sparks . . . I believe she'll do."

And he disappeared into the night.

She was given a new bed, away from the mud on Mr. Bruno's plantation. She didn't have to haunt the barrack-bungalows. She lived at the main compound, high on a hill. She had a cook to boil her eggs and fix her porridge in the morning. She sat at a table with Sparks and Mr. Bruno.

"We're depending on you, daughter. We'll give you a cover story, but stick to the truth as much as you can. Ruben's lads will make contact. He won't desert a cousin out of his own childhood. All the coca barons have an absolutely pristine sense of justice . . . the trick is to find you a legend that isn't too outrageous . . . Sparks, shall we make her a nurse?"

"No, sir. An American nurse who happens to land in Ruben's own city?"

"But he won't consider her a gringa. Her people are Colombian . . . daughter, where was your mama born?"

"Medellín . . . my father too."

"There! You see. She's gone back to her ancestral village."

"Yes, a village with a homicide rate that's too colossal to

be counted. And our Yolanda on a sentimental journey. It won't wash."

"We could turn her into a cocaine bunny from Nueva York."

"She'd be dead within five minutes, Ruben or no Ruben. You had it right the first time, sir. Stick to the truth. She's a Christian Commando, looking for King Ruben to cut a deal with him. Not coca. Not dollars. But trees."

"Ah, the daughter reveals herself, plays her only trump card, with all the other agencies lurking about. The antidrug units don't like us. The secret police consider us Communists. And the DEA will shit a brick if we land a girl in Medellín."

"They'd see it as another one of our quixotic assaults. A cowgirl in cocaine country. They'll let her pass right through their lines. They'll assume we have White House clearance on this."

"And what if they bother to check?"

"The White House will do what it always does. It won't confirm or deny. And we'll be sitting pretty with Yolanda in the Parque Bolivar . . . it'll work, Bruno, if we don't jazz it up."

"Then shall we brief the girl, for God's sake?"

"After dinner," Sparks said, sucking on a ham bone.

Yolanda felt like she was in an asylum. But two civilian generals had adopted her. And she was rather short on papas these days.

An enormous truck arrived at the compound. Men began to unload it while Yolanda ate. She saw strange cardboard buildings that were Yolanda's own size. A whole city was assembled on the far side of the mess hall, with parks and bridges, barrios and gringo hotels. The men were artisans of some kind. Because they could sculpt a city out of painted boards. They hammered, nailed, produced tufts of grass, combing each bit of landscape as they progressed. Yolanda didn't have to close her eyes to imagine what city it was. The artisans had made Medellín for her. She'd never watched a city grow like that in all her life. She'd arrived at the door of enchantment and she didn't want to go back.

5

"I SWIPED IT from the Defense Department," Bruno said, walking her through Medellín. "Every street is exactly to scale. That was in the good old days of the Strategic Air Command. The secretary of the Air Force wanted an image-perfect model of every town on earth with a population over one mil. He was a stickler for accuracy, that man. He had his fly boys stand in the heart of a town, in case the bombs had to fall. I loved that man. He was one of a kind, Secretary Stevens. He passed away . . . and I inherited this model of Medellín, even though it isn't really mine."

Yolanda was on the Avenida Oriental, near the big cathedral and the Hotel Rumania, with its pink curtains. Medellín's skyscrapers were enormous white and brown teeth. The hills around the city had been carpentered into little cluttered terraces that looked like dancing ribbons of red and green. It was all cardboard and papier-mâché, but she'd never felt so involved with a town. This crazy model was calling to her.

Yolanda, ayude los desamparades de Medellín. Ayude, Yolanda.

And Yolanda began to wonder if she were some kind of witch. She followed Mr. Bruno across the plains of Medellín, trying to absorb as many buildings and streets as she could. She was on Calle 54.

"The locals have their own names for the numbered streets. Fifty-four is the Avenida Caracas. Study this old model, daughter, or you might get lost."

"I'm studying hard as I can."

And Yolanda worked at memorizing the path of each little highway, the bend of a street, the marketplaces, the hotels, like the Pichincha, the Odeón, and the Europa Normandie, the cemeteries, the churches, until she had most of Medellín right inside her belly.

"Did your mama tell you stories of Medellín?"

"No, Mr. Bruno . . . she was working all the time. And my papa died before he could tell a lot of stories."

"What about your ancestors, eh? Are they from Medellín, like your mama and papa?"

"I think so . . . one or two might have come from Bogotá. I'm not sure. I was never good at history."

"Criollos, eh?"

"Sí," said Yolanda, like a little girl.

"Then you don't even know about your strange ancestry."

"All ancestries are strange, señor."

"But Medellín's ancestors are stranger than most. The original settlers were very private people. They wouldn't keep slaves or bother about other settlements. The cathedral had a curious design. The nave was slightly twisted . . . there could have been another secret church inside the cathedral. Perhaps a synagoga, eh? Suppose the settlers were hebreos, running from the Inquisition . . . then it all makes sense.

They wouldn't intermarry with Indios or slaves they never had. These isolatos didn't traffic with merchants from other towns. They divided the territory they had into small farms, and soon they had their own little society of strange men, hidalgos who bargained among themselves . . . and followed whatever decrees arrived from the kings of Spain. Some metamorphosis must have taken place among the Jewish hidalgos. Their synagoga was buried deeper and deeper inside the cathedral. Crosses appeared in the cemeteries. They brought over Christian wives from Mother Spain and began to buy and sell slaves. And Medellín was a quiet town until the coffee boom of nineteen hundred and three. It seems the world couldn't survive without a cup of Colombian coffee. With coffee you got the skyscrapers. And in the seventies you got cocaine. Modern Medellín, home of coffee and coca 'beans.' But the new hidalgos have the same love of independence and isolation. They don't like outsiders. Medellín has its own airline, its own politics, its own army, run by the narcotraficantes, of course. Its own hacienda for the poor, financed by your cousin, Don Ruben . . . I'm curious if he has some hebreo blood."

Yolanda didn't know what to think about the clandestino Jews of Medellín. She was a girl who'd always gone to Mass. Priests were holy men. And even if Benjamin was a bastardo, Yolanda intended to raise him as a Catholic if she could. She had nothing against the rabinos of Brooklyn, Manhattan, and the Bronx, but she did not feel tied to them, unless it was some big secret in her life. Her mama always said the rosary, and how could she tell if her papa had had some longing for the rabinos? She could barely remember his face.

"I'm not sure about Ruben," she said. "But I don't think he was a rabino when he was nine."

And she pushed deeper into Medellín, until the boss of the Christian Commandos was far behind, engulfed in some lost avenue, while Yolanda could drink up the different skyscrapers . . . until she believed that Medellín was her home, not Nueva York.

"Benjamin," she muttered, because crazy as she was, caught in an enchanted cardboard town, she might forget her own boy.

"What about the desamparades?" she yelled across the valley of skyscrapers.

"Which desamparades, daughter?"

"The homeless ones of Medellín."

"Not to worry," Mr. Bruno said. "Everybody's homeless in Medellín . . . now get some sleep."

6

SHE DIDN'T stay very long in that little hermitage on the hill. When she woke up, Medellín wasn't there. The streets, the parks, the skyscrapers were gone. She wondered if she could have dreamt the whole thing. What if Mr. Bruno's gang were a bunch of mind benders? And Yolanda was their little zombie girl. But she had faith in her old professor, Melvin P. Sparks, who arrived in his black limousine and shooed Yolanda out of there before she could have a proper breakfast.

"Professor Sparks, I'm not moving until I have my morning egg."

"You little hen, can't you see? The cook is on a holiday. Nobody's here."

"But they had to come pretty early to pack up the cardboard town."

"What cardboard town?"

"Medellín."

"Jesus, did you fall for that crap of Bruno's. *His* Medellín is twenty years old."

"Well, I learned a lot," she said.

"Girl, I'm leading you out to the very edge. You'll be walking point for the Christian Commandos. You'll be taking arrows in the chest. What's that model going to do for you? The cartel's renamed half the streets. They're selling electricity and drinking water. They're creating corpses by the minute. They're buying up dollars, because the peso isn't worth a bean. You know what a lone woman is worth in Medellín? Nada, sweetheart. Nothing at all."

"Then why are you sending me in?"

"Because you are our last resort. If our side keeps banging up the jungle, searching for Ruben's labs, we won't have a goddamn rain forest in Colombia . . . or the whole of South America, because that Ruben has a mighty long arm. He could set up shop in Bolivia or Brazil. What the hell are borders to a cocaine king?"

"And so I arrive and Ruben's men come waltzing up to me and take me into the jungle. Am I supposed to sleep with him, like a good little Christian Commando? Is that what it's all about? Am I your putita, Professor Sparks?"

"Jesus, I don't know."

"What if Ruben decides not to find me in Medellín?"

"Oh, he'll find you," Sparks said.

"Why are you so sure?"

"Because every spy in Medellín will have your dossier."

"Where will they get it from?"

"From me, girl. They'll get it from me."

She was put on a plane at some goddamn military base. All she saw were soldiers. But there weren't soldiers on the plane. Just Sparks and another man. He looked like an hombre with Indian blood. He had a small mustache. His nails were manicured. He wore two gold watches on his wrist. His green eyes seemed to stare out at Yolanda from inside some dark turret. Sparks introduced him as General Muzo Martinez, comandante of the Colombian Air Force and acting minister of justice. The comandante kissed her hand.

"Welcome to my country."

She didn't mind the hand kissing as much as the green eyes, which wouldn't let go of Yolanda. But she had to break the spell of that ballsy little son of a bitch. "General, we haven't come to your country yet."

"Ah, but this airplane is part of Colombia, no?"

"Sí," Yolanda said.

"Muzo," Sparks said, "the girl is a paisa, like you. Her mama and papa were born in Medellín."

The comandante kissed her hand again.

"Then I welcome you home to the home you have never seen."

There was a little fridge on the plane, and the comandante kept pulling out bottles of beer. He opened the bottles with his teeth. The ice began to go from his green eyes. He was just another general who couldn't stop kissing Yolanda's hand. He belched, excused himself, and wandered into the toilet.

Yolanda whispered into Sparks's ear. "If that man's our friend, I wonder who our enemies are?"

"What's wrong with Muzo?"

"Well, for one thing, he's comandante of the Colombian Air Force."

"Don't concern yourself with titles. Muzo's an environmentalist, like us. And he belongs to Ruben's political party."

"Next thing you'll tell me is he smuggles cocaine for the cartel."

"Yes, he has . . . on occasion. But he's also napalmed Ruben's laboratories. He can't escape his country's politics. He's a civil servant. That's why he'd like to see Ruben in some neutral corner before the damn country destroys itself."

"Is a jungle grave neutral enough?" Yolanda asked.

"Don't be silly. He's an honorable man. Besides, he's on our payroll. He thinks he's working for the president of the United States."

"In other words, he's one more simple soldier, like me."

The comandante returned from the toilet.

"Muzo, the señorita is worried about your bona fides. She thinks you might betray her little cousin. She asks why she should trust you."

"She doesn't require an intermediary," Muzo said. "She can ask for herself."

"She's shy around strangers," Sparks said.

Yolanda couldn't tell who was worse, the hand-kissing comandante or the professor with that silky mouth of his.

"He's right," Yolanda said. "I can talk. I have my own tongue . . . I am suspicious, General. Did the professor tell you I'm a convicted bank robber? I never even got to graduate from Harrington Hills. The professor yanked me right out. And I'm on a fool's mission, if you ask me. I don't want the little cousin to get hurt. I haven't seen him for centuries. But he's still part of my clan."

"Bravo," the comandante said. "Would you feel more comfortable, señorita, if I was with some environmental commission? Medellín doesn't have one. It doesn't even have an environment. But we do have a Green Party. I am its secretary general. And Don Ruben is with the Greens. A contradiction, eh? A traficante who is also a Green. But this is la vida medellín."

"And how do I fit into la vida?"

"Very much. Don Ruben is a little crazy right now. He trusts no one. He has his private police . . . and a price on his head. The narcopolicía, the very ones he bribed, want to kill him. He has become a very expensive toy. So he hires doubles, and all the doubles die. Yet he never lacks volunteers. There's still a lot of romance in playing Don Ruben for a month or a week. He is our hero, the gringo boy who came to us from Nueva York . . . like you."

"But how do I fit in?"

"He will not be able to resist meeting you, señorita. I know Ruben. He has a terrible curiosity . . . I heard him talk about you, more than once."

"Now I get the picture. You convinced the Christian Commandos to spring me. It was all your idea."

"Sí," the comandante said. "It was my idea. I asked Mel to track you down. It took months. We only had a first name. *Yolanda.* And here you are. With me and Mel. That is the magic of modern communication. I had my own technicians search for you. See how clever we are in Medellín?"

"Clever and crazy."

"Sí. But I am a general. And you should show respect . . . niña, you are the one who can save our city, only you."

The comandante closed his eyes and fell asleep. Yolanda didn't have to guess where her next asylum would be. She'd gone to bed with a bunch of lunatics.

TRANQUILANDIA

7

SHE WAS near a window. Sparks or the comandante must have put a blanket around her. She saw some kind of red mist under the clouds. Medellín. The mist grew. The comandante's plane crept under the clouds and Yolanda saw a city of red roofs in the bowl of a mountain. There were dark patterns of pine trees and more red roofs at the edges of the bowl. And Yolanda realized that the heart of Medellín was like that model she'd seen: a little Manhattan of long brown and white teeth.

The plane landed at an airport far from Little Manhattan. Yolanda was next to the pine trees. There were no other planes around. She wondered if a comandante could merit his own airport. Sparks didn't brief her at all. He handed her a passport, a tourist card, and a letter of introduction from the president of the United States. The envelope had three little words on it. "The White House." Her hands started to shake.

"It's not a forgery, girl."

"Well, why is the president introducing me to people? I never met the man."

"It's done all the time," Sparks said. "It's a matter of protocol. Bruno and I politicked for the letter. We had to piss blood, but we got it. You're our 'man' in Medellín."

"I'm nobody's 'man,' Professor Sparks. I came out of my mama's belly with a fork between my legs. And if you can't tell the difference, find yourself another one of Ruben's cousins to play with."

"Don't be so goddamn literal," Sparks said, and he and the comandante started to laugh.

"Niña, you should relax."

"How and where, General? In your bed? I'm not your putita. Remember that."

"Que putería," the comandante said. "She is worse than a zambo."

"What's a zambo?" Yolanda asked.

"A negrito with Indian blood."

Neither Muzo nor Sparks accompanied her into Medellín.

"You're on your own, girl."

"But how do I contact you? With secret ink or something?"

"We'll be in touch," Sparks said.

"What about money and maps?"

"It's all in your kit, girl."

Sparks put Yolanda's suitcase into a battered Oldsmobile that served as the airport limousine. The driver couldn't keep his eyes off Yolanda. He looked like a crackhead from Yolanda's own barrio. His name was ChiChi. He was a zambo who also had some Chinese blood.

"How long have you been working for the general?" she asked.

"Not long."

They kept passing checkpoints on the road from the air- port. She saw mean-looking soldiers in black berets. But ChiChi didn't have to stop once. Yolanda realized that the zambo had been working for the general a long, long time, perhaps as long as Yolanda had been alive. She began to hear little pops in the distance, like wet firecrackers, and then the pops grew louder until Yolanda's ears ached from all the noise.

"They're bombs, aren't they?"

"Sí," the zambo said.

"Who's exploding them?"

"Taita's people."

"And who the hell is Taita?"

"Don Ruben. He's papa to all the campesinos."

"Have you ever met Ruben?"

"Many times. But you cannot always tell his doubles from Don Ruben. They rob for him, they marry chicas in Ruben's name, they die for him. It has become an entire industry, being Ruben's double. Ten or twenty are born each day."

"Sounds like a scam," Yolanda said. "Everybody's trying to cash in on the situation."

"But it has a political efficacy. You cannot kill a man who has so many doubles. It would take five years to sort out the real Ruben. And even then it would only be a guess."

"Then how does he rule?"

"With his wits, mamzelle . . . and coca dollars."

Yolanda heard another one of the firecrackers.

"What are Taita's people bombing today?"

"Police barracks. Radio stations. Movie theaters that belong to the government."

"The government owns the movie theaters?"

"In Medellín, sí."

"And what does Ruben own?"

"Radio stations. Movie theaters. And the barracks for his private police."

"And does the government bomb them too?"

"Very often."

"ChiChi," Yolanda said. "I think I'm going to love your town."

"This is not my town, mamzelle. I was born in Barranquilla, where they do not hate the zambos."

"Then why are you here?"

"Because I am in Muzo's debt."

"What does that mean?"

"Mean, mamzelle? It is very clear. Muzo would have disemboweled me and all my children if I left his employ."

"But aren't you in the air force?"

ChiChi smiled into the Oldsmobile's dirty mirror. "You shouldn't mock me, mamzelle. A zambo cannot volunteer or be inducted. We are nurses to the military, nothing more. The general saved my life. He rescued me from one of the guerrilla bands. The guerrillas are always kidnapping zambos. I don't know why. We can never pay the ransom price. But Muzo paid it. And so I am in his debt."

"Then you ought to be glad," Yolanda said. "At least you had a ransomer."

"Sí."

The zambo took her to Tranquilandia, a suburb Ruben had built for the poor of Medellín. There had been an earlier Tranquilandia, a cocaine finca the traficantes had built in Los Llanos, the great plains between the Andes and the Orinoco. That Tranquilandia had its own airport, electricity, and flag. It was like a separate country that produced cocaine. It had sixteen laboratories and an official permit from the guerrillas who controlled much of the great plains. With its guerrilla bodyguards, Tranquilandia became the biggest cocaine factory in the world. But then a new broom arrived in Bogotá, Rodrigo Lara Bonilla, minister of justice, who declared war on the traficantes. He raided Tranquilandia with ten thousand troops. He seized airplanes and entire laboratories and tossed fifteen tons of pure cocaine into the Rio Yari. The traficantes fought back. They bombed the Palace of Justice. They murdered Rodrigo. But they could no longer build such a magnificent finca to produce their cocaine. The iguanas had come to Bogotá, Drug Enforcement people who belonged to Uncle Sam. They teamed up with local iguanas, the Securidad, and started to dismantle all the coca labs they could find. The traficantes ran to Panama and Peru. But Don Ruben didn't believe in exile. He wouldn't give up his barrios for the iguanas. He hid his fincas deeper and deeper in the Amazon, and built a new Tranquilandia, a barrio in the hills of Medellín, with a hospital, a church, a movie theater, a skating rink, cheap hotels called hospedajes, and a rumbeadero, where his followers could stage tango contests on Wednesday nights, in honor of Taita, who was born on a Wednesday. Don Ruben was the last big traficante. The Securidad killed and killed, but it couldn't seem to get rid of Ruben, or Ruben's ghosts.

And Yolanda entered Tranquilandia while it was in a state of siege. The iguanas were everywhere. Colonel Isadoro Jacob, chief of the Medellín Securidad, who helped discover the first Tranquilandia and destroy the traficantes, one by one, had promised Muzo to deliver Ruben, without any ghosts. He cut off the electricity and water supply in all the barrios of Medellín that were loyal to Taita. And Taita's men bombed the Medellín Stock Exchange and closed the financial district. Medellín was running out of food *and* money. And Taita's doubles still danced in all the Wednesday night tangos in Medellín.

Yolanda lived at the Hotel Suez, a hospedaje on Candle Street, which was cluttered with checkpoints and closed to traffic. It didn't take long for Yolanda to learn that the Hotel Suez was a part-time brothel, and that the street itself was in the middle of a red-light district, called Candelaria. But the niñas had very little to do. Medellín was in a crisis, and the only ones who had money were the iguanas. The girls were devout rubenistas, and often they would not sleep with the iguanas, who would arrest them and oblige the girls to become prostitutas at their own police barracks. And so any girl who displeased the iguanas might disappear and add to the army of desamparades in Medellín. Sometimes the iguanas also disappeared. And then there would be terrible all-night searches of Candelaria. The brothelkeepers were forced to pay fines with money they didn't have. More girls disappeared. It was a cruel business, Medellín.

Yolanda was in the thick of a civil war. The day after she arrived on Candle Street, the iguanas knocked on her door. Two men in enormous sportscoats and black neckerchiefs. They looked like sinister clowns. They carried assault rifles on their shoulders and had green toothpicks in their mouths. They wanted Yolanda to lie down with them. Because she was new and didn't have the sullen look of Candelaria, they offered to pay her in dollars rather than pesos, which lost value minute by minute.

"I'm not a whore," she said.

The iguanas smiled. "Que putería!" they said and kept hurling crumpled dollar bills at Yolanda.

"Nueva York, eh? . . . niña norteamericana."

They began to touch her breasts. The iguanas stank of beer. They grabbed at Yolanda as if she were their own private cow. They didn't have much seduction in their eyes. They were bored and excited and lazy. They pulled on their neckerchiefs. Yolanda was scared, because she had nothing to bargain with, except her body. But she had graduated from boot camp. She slapped the tallest iguana on the mouth and showed him her letter from the president of the United States.

The stationary seized their interest. The iguanas had never seen such white paper. They couldn't decide whether to kill Yolanda first and then read the letter. But she was a little too pretty to finish off, just like that. Still, they would have to punish this niña from New York for slapping a member of the Securidad.

They knew enough English to recognize the signature of a president. They started to laugh in a skittish way. They wanted to make a fotocopia of the letter, but they did not dare. They had to distance themselves from this puta and her presidente. "La novia," they said. "La novia del presidente."

They returned the letter. They clicked their heels and

forgot that they were no longer wearing military boots. They were Securidad, but they'd never even been to Bogotá. They were raised in the slums of Medellín. The only language they'd ever learned was the language of pistoleros and the police. They weren't clever enough to become traficantes. And they couldn't understand the rhetoric of guerrilla priests, who talked of giving up their own bread, bricks, and blood for the campesinos, or working without wages. That was comunista talk.

"Ah," they said. "Yolanda Ramirez. The president's little bride."

They kissed her on the cheek, saluted Yolanda to hide their own fear, pulled on the neckerchiefs, and got out of that hospedaje, the Hotel Suez.

8

WHAT COULD she say about this putería of a country? Yolanda felt lost. She wasn't really equipped to be an environmental commando. And there wasn't much future for bank robbers in Medellín. The banks had no money. The "kit" Sparks had given her was a suitcase full of five-dollar bills. She couldn't leave the kit in her room. The maids or the Suez's Mamá Grande would have seized that swollen money pouch. She had to pin it between her legs like a chastity belt, or the thieves of Tranquilandia would have lured it out of her.

She could hardly walk into the streets. There was so much hunger around her. The niños had swollen bellies. Their mamas had pale, runny eyes. She began to distribute some of the five-dollar bills. But she had to be judicious, or the whole of Candelaria would have arrived at her door.

So she dug five-dollar bills under the aprons of the worst-looking mamas and scurried home to her hospedaje. It was a mean and miserable life. The markets didn't have one tomato. The corn looked like toothless stumps. The flour, whatever there was of it, was all wormy. The food in all of Candelaria couldn't have raised a family of dwarfs. But there were dollarias that could get you what you wanted if you had the right currency. Charlotte russes. Wine. Videos. An airplane even. Currency was king. Yolanda didn't like to shop at the dollarias. They were run by the Securidad as a kind of black market. But she didn't have much of a choice. She would have starved in Medellín, like most people.

Each dollar was worth a thousand Colombian pesos, and every morning and afternoon the value of the peso dropped, but there was such a shortage of currency and such despair, that merchants would only accept dollars and deutsche marks, and soon dollars and deutsche marks were so scarce, that traders would cut the bills in half and double the supply. But it brought Yolanda no pleasure to be a rich girl in Medellín.

One afternoon she sat at the soda fountain inside the dollaria and ordered a banana split. It had always been a dream of Yolanda's, ever since she was a little girl, that she would grow up in the barrio and live on a diet of café con leche and banana splits. Banana splits had been her idea of gringa heaven. But she couldn't enjoy all that milk and cream in Medellín. She left her split at the counter and walked out of the dollaria. People thought she was crazy.

They called her "la novia del presidente." They all knew about her white letter in the white envelope. She couldn't stay anonymous very long. But all her notoriety didn't bring her much closer to Ruben. Her cousin never called. And even if he was hiding in the Amazon, he might have left a message for her through one of his doubles. Perhaps he had no respect for a girl who shopped at the dollaria and ordered a banana split. Then she remembered that he was the coca king and probably received a tax from all the dollarias in his districts.

And so she lived this seesaw existence of Commando and rich girl with nothing to do. And all the while she waited for Taita to knock on her door. She would have welcomed a visit from her old college professor or that general from the Colombian Air Force or that zambo who belonged to the general for life. But no one came, not even the iguanas, who were frightened of her now. She was like a leper in a colony of putas and poor people.

The skating rink was closed. The Cine del Hollywood Sud only accepted dollars and deutsche marks, and so Yolanda would sit in a darkened movie theater with one or two other patrons and watch *The Maltese Falcon* dubbed into a Spanish that didn't make much sense. Still, it was better than nothing, and since the Cine del Hollywood Sud had its own generator, there were no electricity problems, and she could fall into the dream of a film and try to make sense out of some falcon that was as elusive as her very own life.

And there was always Humphrey Bogart, or El Bogey, as the Cine liked to call its favorite star. Bogey in black and white, talking some crazy Spanish in the middle of the afternoon, when San Francisco itself could have been a suburb of Medellín. But she couldn't hide in a movie theater. And on her third Wednesday in Tranquilandia, she visited the rumbeadero where Taita's men held their tango contests. The rumbeadero was at the other end of Candle Street. It was called El Rey, in honor of the tango king, Guillermo Gaudí, whose plane had crashed in the mountains over Medellín in 1945. The population had never recovered. Fifty years after the accident, people could evoke El Maestro, who danced with all the danger of a matador. His picture was on the front wall of the rumbeadero. He looked like a bird of prey.

It was here, in the rumbeadero El Rey, that the citizens of Tranquilandia assembled. It was sacred ground. The iguanas had never made an arrest inside the rumbeadero. It would have started a revolution. There was already a reign of terror outside in the streets. But iguanas danced with rubenistas in El Rey. The campesinos had their own marketplace and church. They could light a candle for a dead hero. They could exchange stories, show both halves of a dollar bill that their mujeres had ironed for them. And they could sit in the balcony, sip small cups of coffee with a lot of milk, watch the tango dancers and dream of Guillermo Gaudí, who never deserted them for Hollywood or Manhattan. He wasn't a fashionable dancer, Don Guillermo. He presided over the birth of the tango in Medellín, when it was a ritualized knife fight in the barrios, between two men who "tangoed" with each other's women after each thrust of the knife. Guillermo never lost that violent edge. He was the knife when he danced in the rumbeaderos of Medellín. He had a body that could wound. And all his tangos were preparations for a kill.

This is what Yolanda saw, men and women dancing like El Rey had danced, with merciless thrusts of their bodies, bite after bite, until she nearly swooned, because there was no dancing like that in her own barrio. And she didn't feel alone.

But she started to shiver. Men appeared on the floor of the rumbeadero in white scarves and high-heeled shoes that were favored in the barrios. They didn't present themselves as a small family with one face. But she could tell that these were Ruben's doubles. The campesinos clapped. "Taita, Taita!" She recognized her cousin in none of the clowns. They were impersonators, comedians on a dance floor. It was hard to believe that such men would have died for Ruben, or anyone else. They were benefiting from all the doubles around Ruben, and had become the doubles of doubles.

It sickened Yolanda to watch them dance.

She drank a café con leche and returned to the Suez.

9

December 12, 1994

Dear Professor Sparks,

I have tried to be a good Commando. But I don't know how. I have a weakness for banana splits. I'm not sure how long I will have the strength to keep out of the dollaria. One day I will gorge myself and that will be the end.

Your devoted pupil,
(signed) Yolanda Ramirez

SHE LOST blood over that letter. None of her words seemed right. And she didn't even have an address for Sparks. All she had was a chastity belt of five-dollar bills and recollections of Ruben as a little boy. So she scribbled the one address she knew: Melvin P. Sparks, c/o the Christian Commandos, Washington, D.C., Los Estados Unidos. She couldn't find a mailbox on Candle Street. So she brought the letter to the dollaria and mailed it from the airline counter for ninety-five cents. And she fed five-dollar bills to starving women outside the dollaria.

She went upstairs and heard someone singing in her room at the Suez. She opened the door. An iguana was sitting in her chair. He had the same black neckerchief, but this iguana wore white boots. And he didn't have a silly sportscoat. He must have been a captain of the guard, or comandante of the Medellín barracks, some little chief of the Securidad. He didn't say hello. He kept on singing a song about Guillermo Gaudí.

> Maestro, why did you go to your mountain
> And leave us all alone?
> Poor children of the tango
> Without your difficult, devouring love.

Yolanda wouldn't interrupt his singing, but as soon as he stopped, she said, "I am la novia del presidente. I can do you a lot of harm."

He laughed. "You are the bruja of Candle Street."

"I can show you my letter," she said.

"I also have a letter," he told her. And this little chief of the Securidad took out of his pocket the letter she had sent to Professor Sparks.

"Where did you get this? . . . you lousy thief."

She grabbed at the letter, but he kept escaping Yolanda's hand. He put on a pair of gold-rimmed spectacles and perused the letter.

"So you adore ice cream sodas."

"Banana splits," she said.

"Chinga, they are the same."

"Where were you born, señor? There are no bananas in an ice cream soda."

"Ah, then you haven't tried a soda medellín. You would quickly change your mind."

"What is it you want?"

He took out of his other pocket a small bundle of five-dollar bills that had been neatly ironed.

"You are not Nuestra Señora. You are a witch. You cannot offer us charity. You have not earned that right and you never will."

"Who are you?"

"Colonel Isadoro Jacob of the Securidad."

"That sounds like a Jewish name," she said.

"I am a follower of Jesus."

"But your family name could have been Jewish . . . like the first hidalgos of Medellín."

"A fairy tale."

"Why are you so sure?"

"Because I am descended from priests who took off the cloth to become conquistadors. We are all fighters in my family. We dance the tango and we also kill."

"Like Guillermo Gaudí."

"Chinga, have you seen one rabino in Medellín."

She hadn't, Yolanda had to admit, though she had searched as hard as she could. "They could be wearing disguises."

"This is not the Inquisition."

"It's pretty close," she said. "People starve . . . and you have dollarias for the rich."

"And you are a Commando of Señor Professor Sparks. A Christian soldier. Isn't that also an inquisition?"

"We're environmentalists," she said. "We don't kill."

"Liar! Didn't you arrive on a plane with General Muzo? Do you know how many campesinos he has butchered? And he has his own personal assassin who dropped you off in Candelaria."

"ChiChi? He's a zambo. He can't even get into the Colombian Air Force."

"Idiota! He's a captain in Muzo's private police. He kills for Muzo . . . almost every day."

"But I thought the guerrillas kidnapped him . . . and General Muzo paid the ransom."

"A fairy tale."

"Everything's a fairy tale in Medellín. Zambos and Jews. Guillermo Gaudí."

The colonel rose up from the chair to slap Yolanda.

"You mustn't say that about El Maestro. He is the one god we all agree on . . . Guillermo never betrayed us. I am sorry, bruja. I shouldn't have touched your face."

Her nose started to bleed, and Colonel Jacob took out an elaborate silk handkerchief, stooped over Yolanda, and wiped away the blood. And there was something about his catlike motions, his agility in and out of her own chair, that bothered Yolanda. She'd seen that agility before . . . in a little boy from her own barrio.

"You're Ruben," she said.

"Don't be ridiculous."

"You're Ruben. And it's unkind of you, cousin, to treat me like a stranger."

"I'm not your cousin."

"You are. You can call yourself Colonel Jacob until your nose falls off, but you're Ruben Falcone, the outlaw, the smuggler, the builder of barrios, and my little cousin."

"I'm older than you are."

"But you were always a shrimp . . . and you're as feeble as your doubles, who are cowards and unbearable men."

"Isadoro" removed his spectacles and returned them to a silver case.

"I tried to discourage all that impersonation. But it happens. There were thousands of Guillermos in Guillermo's day."

"But Guillermo's doubles didn't have to die."

"They did. In knife fights and civil wars."

"I don't care about Guillermo. I haven't seen you in a century. How come you haven't kissed me, cousin?"

"Because I am not convinced yet that I want to kiss some bruja of the Christian Commandos."

"I told you. We're environmentalists."

"Yes. You're also El Presidente's soldiers. You get him out of embarrassing situations."

"I'm your cousin Yolanda. We played doctor in the basement of your mama's house. We were engaged. You promised to marry me."

He smiled. "You should never believe a boy of nine."

"You're the bruja. You're the witch. Why did you abandon me?"

"Jesus, I was just out of kindergarten. I couldn't control my fate. My papa returned to Medellín. Was I supposed to take you along?"

"Yes . . . who is Colonel Jacob?"

"Comandante of Medellín's Securidad. He's been trying to massacre me for months."

"Is he hebreo?"

"Perhaps we all are . . . I don't know. They like to say in the tourist brochures that we're hebreos. It's romantic. A lost tribe. There's no evidence. There's no proof. I told you. Jacob is descended from conquistadors. He has dueling scars on his face. He's a cabrón."

"Then why do you impersonate him?"

"Because it infuriates Don Isadoro. And I had to have some disguise. But why are you here?"

"To find you for the Commandos," she said. "They want to save the Amazon . . . they want to make a deal."

"Is that what they told you, cousin? They are the destroyers, not me. But I have become an embarrassment to Uncle Sam. The traficante who is saluted by Greenpeace. There are no cars in Candelaria because I have banned them."

"Cousin, there is also no food."

"Because Muzo keeps the sweet potatoes for his own men. I hijack his milk trucks. I kidnap members of his family."

"And you trade drugs."

"Sí. That is our economy. That is our crop. Should I grow coffee? Then Muzo would get rich. Because he controls the coffee prices."

"Ruben," Yolanda said, "come home with me to a Hundred and Twenty-ninth Street. I'll introduce you to the crackheads who smoke your cocaine. They're zombies, Ruben. They steal. They shiver. They die."

"I didn't create them, little sister. I have nothing to do with crackheads. I have a product everybody wants, including the policemen and the generals who try to deprive me of my crops. If I go down, Yolanda, Muzo will sit in my place. He would be the traficante."

"But Muzo isn't my cousin. You are. And your laboratories are ruining the rain forests."

"Is that what they told you? Poor girl. I haven't cut down a single tree. I have laboratories, yes, and coca farms in the forest. How else could I avoid the general? Should I let him close all my fincas? I'm not his fool. He murders Indians, makes war on the guerrillas, and blames it all on Ruben. He wants the coca. He wants all the trees. And I am his battle cry. 'Kill the last traficante!' "

"But the general told me that you were allies once upon a time, that you belonged to the same political party. The Greens."

"Yes, little sister. We owned a newspaper together. We built sanctuaries for the Huitoto tribesmen. We protected them from the crazy rubber merchants and gold miners. He was also on my payroll once upon a time. He made deliveries for me. He protected my runners. But I am out of fashion with the Yankee conquistadors. And now Muzo would like to forget our mutual history. The Yankees want me dead. The Commandos would like to trade my skin so the jungles can breathe again. And I will have to lose. But I will die on my own terms, little sister."

Ruben got up from his chair. "I'd better go."

"You haven't kissed me yet."

"I am in a somber mood."

"But why would they bring me here, Ruben, if they hadn't heard you talking about me? I was sitting in jail."

"I know. I could have gotten you out. It would only have cost me a million or a million and a half . . . I was missing you, little sister."

"After twenty years?"

"Why not? I've grown sentimental. Kill me for it . . ."

He kissed Yolanda on the mouth, and it wasn't a cousinly kiss. And then he ran out of the room, like Guillermo Gaudí at the end of a tango.

10

YOLANDA DIDN'T have time to think. The zambo appeared at her door ten minutes after Ruben's departure. She felt like a train station all of a sudden, with little men coming and going. This little man was carrying a pistol with a long "silenciador." He didn't look like Muzo's orphan any more. He had a silk blouse against his burnt amber skin. The sadness had gone out of his eyes.

"ChiChi, do you always come courting with a pistol in your hand?"

"Where's Taita, mamzelle?"

"You must have met him in the street."

"He didn't go down into the street. I would have seen him. Taita is fond of rooftops."

"But how did you know he was here?"

"We were expecting him, mamzelle."

"But how did you know?"

"Your room is one big microphone. That's why we selected this hotel. The Suez is our own little station."

"And your soldiers listened to our entire talk?"

"Sí, mamzelle."

She tried to slap the zambo, but he stepped around her like a matador. He could have been another tango dancer.

"Tell me again how the guerrillas kidnapped you, and the general paid your ransom."

"It is a true story, mamzelle."

"And your loyalty to Muzo makes you an asesino."

"I am Muzo's bodyguard and his chauffeur."

"And a captain in the secret police."

"You shouldn't always listen to a traficante. He likes to exaggerate."

"If you'd found Ruben, would you have killed him in this room?"

"He's much too valuable to kill. We want Ruben alive."

"Then why do you bring an assassin's toy?"

"As a precaution, mamzelle. I might have had to shoot him in the leg. And I would have preferred as little noise as possible."

"God, and to think I might have betrayed him to you . . . Yolanda, you are out of your mind."

"No, no. You are a cautious girl. I admire you, mamzelle."

"ChiChi, are all zambos like you? Do they lie and lie for their generals."

"Mamzelle," he said, "I am a particular case." He took a two-way radio out of his belt, pressed a button, and started to sing. "Zambo Man to Doughboy Two, do you read me, Doughboy?"

Then she heard the deep static of a second voice. "I read you, Zambo Man."

"The parrot is out of its cage. The parrot is out of its cage. Should I pursue?"

"Negative."

"What about the wallflower? Do you want it?"

"Negative, Zambo Man. Just come home, will you? And climb off this fucking frequency before the piranhas get on our back."

"Who are the piranhas?" Yolanda asked.

"Ruben's people."

Another man arrived. ChiChi saluted him like he was the lord high commissioner of the Andes and the Amazon. It was Professor Sparks. He was wearing some kind of general's shirt and a black beret.

ChiChi left, and Yolanda curtsied to the professor. "Congratulations. You look like one hell of a Christian Commando."

"We have to dress like the locals . . . or we might get mistaken for the other side."

"The piranhas, you mean."

"Shouldn't listen to all that radio talk. The situation's fluid, girl. Anything can happen."

"Sure. Guillermo Gaudí might come alive again and dance the tango at the rumbeadero that carries his name. I'm a bruja, didn't you know that? And you, professor, are a lying louse."

"Shhh," he said, "or you'll wake up all our microphones."

"Is that how you treat one of your Commandos? You bug her room? . . . Jesus, that training was just a joke. I'm not a Commando, am I? I'm one little piece of your arsenal. The girl who can lead you to the head piranha."

"No, you're a Commando . . . my ablest pupil by far."

"Professor, I'm not trading Ruben's life for the possibility

of seeing my son. Benjamin will have to stay put. I'm not
your Judas . . . the zambo was going to kill him, wasn't he?"

The professor began to poke around the room. He stood
on Yolanda's chair, fidgeted with different sockets, until the
microphones were "defused."

"It's a rat race, girl. You can't always pick your partners.
Muzo has his own plans. But he can't afford to zap Ruben,
not right now. The president had taken a personal interest
in your cousin. That makes him immortal, at least for a
while. But we have to start a dialogue with the little son of a
bitch. That's why you're here. No other reason. He trusts
you. And you've got to get him to sit down with our people."

"But who are your people, professor? More piranhas?
Taita says he isn't ruining the rain forests. That's Muzo's job.
So why should I help you?'

"Yolanda, he's not as innocent as he likes to think. Should
I show you Ruben's file? He has his own hit squads. The
zambo used to work for Ruben before he joined up with the
general. It's Colombia, girl. Life is cheap."

"That's your philosophy, Professor, not mine." She started
to cry. "I mean, you're the environmentalist. You ought to
change some things. All I see are putas in the windows,
ironing dollar bills. It's only paper, but they iron and iron
and iron."

🐉

He escorted her downstairs, her hidalgo from Texas, Profes-
sor Sparks. The prostitutas were in their rooms, wearing
bright red dresses for customers who would never come.
They were ironing their paper money. It was the only status

they would have in this endless civil war. They were humming songs to Guillermo Gaudí, waiting for a dead tango dancer to deliver them. He was the patron saint of all the putas in Medellín. And Yolanda herself was becoming haunted by Guillermo's ghost. She could feel his arms around her, in the tango's tight embrace . . .

It was the zambo who drove them out of Candelaria in his Oldsmobile. Yolanda wasn't even sure where they were going. But the professor had proof of Ruben's desecration, his sacrifice of Indian culture to the gods of cocaine, his wholesale burning of villages, his destruction of forest land to camouflage his fincas, his murder of farmers who were a little too neutral. Yolanda believed none of it, but she had to see the "proof."

They drove down from the foothills and into the bowl of Medellín. The streets were strung with Christmas lights. The yellow and red bulbs were everywhere, creating little screens against the skyscrapers. Yolanda wasn't so lonely in Little Manhattan. She liked this city of glass, the marketas, the cafés, the movie houses. Her favorite actor was on the billboards, Mickey Rourke, who was playing a hungry caballero, looking for love.

Yolanda saw soldiers outside every café, checkpoints near the movie houses, tiny sandbagged forts outside office buildings. Little Manhattan had become an armed camp in Medellín's latest civil war. But the soldiers didn't seem to menace anyone. They were almost as decorative as Christmas lights. They flirted with the chicas, practiced tango steps, sang their own sad songs about the death of the tango king. It was Navidad in Medellín, even with the explosion of bombs, the arrests, the lack of running water.

The zambo parked outside Securidad headquarters on the Avenida Junin. It was a red box of a building that looked like an old opera house. Locals called it "Casa del Cristo," because the comandante, Isadoro Jacob, might send you to your Saviour from one of its halls.

The zambo didn't go inside with Yolanda and Sparks. He wasn't welcome at the Securidad. Soldiers in black berets kept saluting Sparks. And she had to wonder if they'd all gone to the same military school. She passed through room after room where women in red aprons were ironing the Securidad's own stash of money. It had to be Medellín's main occupation, ironing dollar bills.

"Yolanda," Sparks said, "Isadoro's a lady's man. He'll flirt with you. Don't cut him off too fast. It could be disastrous for us."

"Professor, should I go with him under his desk?"

"Shouldn't patronize me, girl. I have to live on a fucking tightrope in Medellín. Just don't vex him, that's all."

He stopped in front of the colonel's door.

"Aren't you coming in with me?" Yolanda had to ask.

"No. Isadoro's expecting you. He likes to greet a new lady all on his own. I'll wait out here."

Yolanda knocked once and entered Colonel Jacob's anteroom. A receptionist sneered at her, as if she were one more puta come to iron dollar bills.

"I'm Yolanda Ramirez . . . supposed to see the colonel."

"Sí," the receptionist said. "You can go in, mamzelle."

And Yolanda walked into the colonel's private office, which was smaller than she would have imagined for Medellín's chief of Securidad. It had no diplomas or guns or maps on the wall. Jacob's room was filled with books. He had terrible scars around his eyes. He was very blond, and he didn't look like a torturer, though Yolanda wasn't quite sure how a torturer should look. His mouth was pale. His nose was aristocratic, like those paisas who'd settled here and hadn't mingled with the other races.

He offered her a glass of wine and sat her down in a chair. And he didn't study her shape like some lascivious man. He was much gentler with Yolanda than Sparks or Muzo and her own cousin.

"Is Jacob a Hebrew name?" she said after her second sip of wine.

He didn't laugh or scold her. "Ah, you have heard all the Medellín myths. The paisas are a reclusive people. They had no slaves or Indian wives. But I do not think they were a little colony of secret Jews. No menorahs were ever found . . . or traces of the Jewish Easter. But even if they had been conversos, they accepted Christianity long before they arrived. As for my own name, what does it signify? There was an Isadoro in the court of Ferdinand and Isabella. He was the queen's confessor." The scars seemed to ripple on his face. "You met Ruben this morning. He often pretends to be Colonel Jacob. I am his favorite masquerade. And you are curious about him. I could show you pictures of his atrocities. He has tortured many people. He has offered six thousand dollars for the head of each soldier in the Securidad. I do not have to tell you what six thousand dollars can buy in Medellín."

"Tell me anyway," she said after another sip.

"A finca in the hills. A mujer for life. A family of children and goats."

"And hundreds of ironing boards to iron the dollar bills."

He smiled at her, and for a moment the scars went away. "You have discovered our weakness. In Medellín we only handle dollars that are crisp. It is an ignominia to do otherwise. Perhaps it was a fetishism of our Jewish ancestors, who might have been moneylenders. Everyone irons money in Medellín."

"Even Ruben?"

"Yes. The mujers who work for him in his many fincas."

"What price has he put on your head?"

The colonel filled Yolanda's wine glass.

"You have to consider the inflation. Last year's price was a million deutsche marks. This year it might go to a million and ten . . . though the deutsche mark is getting stronger every day . . . against the dollar, of course. I was not thinking of our own pathetic currency."

"And you are trying to kill Ruben."

"Definitely."

"Because he is a traficante."

"That is not my department. I can tell you that coffee and emeralds cannot keep up with inflation. Your cousin is good for our economy, because coca hasn't yet found a sky that is big enough. And Ruben brings down our national debt. Half his operation is perfectly legal. And he pays his taxes religiously. But he is dangerous. He stirs up the campesinos. He intoxicates the Huitotos and other tribes. He makes alliances with the guerrillas. He dreams of some vast paradise where each peasant will have his own finca and little forest . . . and will run drugs for Ruben. He has to be stopped."

"Before he stops you."

"I am serious. He will only bring death and sadness to

everyone. I want to educate the Indios. I want the campesinos to have their milk. But not an impossible paradise."

"And how can I help? By leading Ruben right to the Securidad?"

"No. By getting him out of the country with your Christian soldiers . . . did you see our Sinfonía de Luces?"

"The Christmas lights?"

"They're not only for Christmas. Guillermo Gaudí died two days before Navidad. So the Sinfonía is a double celebration. For Guillermo and baby Jesus. Our two kings."

"Colonel, how did his plane happen to crash in the mountains over Medellín?"

"That's easy. My grandfather had him killed. He was our local minister of justice and chief of the Securidad."

Yolanda looked at all of Jacob's scars. "Why are you telling me this?"

"So you will put all your myths to bed. Guillermo was our tango man and a very big thief, our first mafioso, long before the traficantes. He had his own peasant army. That's why he refused the Hollywood offers and mocked the nightclubs of Buenos Aires and New York. He could not leave his troops. He put a tax on milk and bread. He danced at the meanest rumbeadero to recruit more and more men. It was all tolerated. He bribed the governor of his own province. He contributed to the Securidad. It was a beautiful arrangement. But the tango dancing must have gone to his brain. He wanted Medellín to break with Colombia and become his own peasant republic. The campesinos who paid his bread and milk tax grew delirious, the very ones he had robbed offered their lives up to El Matador. If only he were bluffing, he would have become a very rich man. The government would have paid a heavy ransom to keep such a king in line. But it wasn't a bluff. He had this stubborn messianic streak. So Grandfather, who worshipped Guillermo, had his plane wired. He didn't have a choice. The tango king would have destroyed Medellín."

"Like Ruben will destroy Medellín if he isn't killed."

"There. You have it. You are the instrument of Ruben's fate. Plead with him to go abroad. I will manage his crops and look after his Indians and all his campesinos. But he must be out of Colombia before the Sinfonía's lights go out, eleven days after Navidad."

❦

Sparks was surprised that Colonel Jacob hadn't proposed to make Yolanda one more of his little novias.

"Girl, look me in the eye and tell me he didn't give you a glass of wine."

"Wine isn't everything," Yolanda said, a little tipsy. "He was as polite as a lamb."

"Must be slipping. Or maybe he can't afford another novia."

Yolanda kept stumbling into walls. She watched the colonel's novias ironing all that paper money in room after room. This Securidad station had its very own mint.

"Melvin," she said, suddenly familiar with her prof. "Did you know that Isadoro's grandfather had Guillermo Gaudí killed."

"Shhh, girl. That's kind of a state secret."

And he had the zambo drive her back to the Candelaria district.

GAUDÍ'S GHOST

11

WHO WAS Yolanda? An ex–bank robber who'd become a lonely cluck in some barrio her cousin had built. Her own little Benjamin belonged to the courts. Her mama and papa were dead. She was the bruja of Chase Manhattan Bank. She had to save Ruben, but she didn't know how. She tried the little post office trick. She scratched a note. *Cousin, meet with me, anywhere.* She put it in an envelope, mailed it in care of the White House, U.S.A., and delivered her letter to the same airline counter at the dollaria, hoping Ruben would get his hands on it.

Nothing happened as far as Yolanda could tell. And while she waited for Don Ruben, she visited with one of the niñas at the Hotel Suez. The niña's name was Rafaela. She was a mulata with pink skin. She ironed her money all day, like the other niñas. But her dollar bills were growing scarce. She was the most beautiful niña Yolanda had ever met. She was full at the hips, but her hands and feet were small, like some kind of mulata princess. She survived because she was one of Isadoro's novias. She visited him at the Securidad twice a week. She'd had a child with Isadoro, a boy who was called Benjamin, like Yolanda's baby. But this Benjamin lived at a special finca in the hills of Medellín, where all the other "love babies" lived, the bastardos of Medellín's aristocracia. The paisas didn't like to part with their children. Isadoro was a benevolent dictator to his entire brood. He had a paisa wife with five paisa children, who would inherit his name and his wealth, but he was almost as fond of the "nameless ones."

"Don't you miss your own little squirrel?" Yolanda said, crying over the sadness of that lost Benjamin in the hills.

"Sure I miss, but I see him at Christmas and Easter. He knows who I am."

It was Isadoro who gave her whatever dollar bills she had.

Yolanda couldn't help herself. She introduced Rafaela to her own terrible addiction for banana splits. The two of them would sit at the dollaria and eat up all the milk and cream with those long spoons that were essential to a banana split.

The iguanas left them alone. Rafaela belonged to Don Isadoro. And Yolanda belonged to Don Ruben and the president of the United States. It was from Rafaela and a few other niñas that Yolanda learned to unravel the life of the tango king. Guillermo Gaudí was born somewhere in the southern districts of Medellín on the eve of World War I. He was a paisa whose parents had amounted to very little. It was the time of the great coffee boom, and Medellín grew from a pueblito paisa into a commercial empire of its own, with banks and textile mills and coffee warehouses. But the little paisa wasn't part of this boom. He could neither read nor write, according to the niñas, and he never would. He signed his name with an enormous *G,* the only letter of the alphabet he'd learned by heart. He had to steal bags of coffee to keep his parents alive. He attended no schools. He worked in the old flower district from the time he was seven. It was cutting flowers and coffee bags that made him agile with a knife.

Tango fever had already hit Medellín. It was the days of Valentino and Blasco Ibáñez. And all the tango "artists" were imported from Argentina . . . or Hollywood. But Guillermo had done his tangoing in the streets. He'd slit a man's throat before he was twelve. He was a father at fourteen. And Guillermo Gaudí took the tango away from the aristocrats. He danced in the upper-class rumbeaderos around the Basilica de la Candelaria, he performed in the fincas of the rich, with his panther's steps, his knife-scarred body, and his dark, unfathomable face. He didn't marry the daughters of coffee merchants, though they pursued him. The Roaring Twenties had arrived in Medellín, just like in the United States, said Rafaela, who chronicled what she could of Guillermo's life.

And the offers came. Hollywood scouts descended upon the city. They were desperate for another Valentino, "a paisa with the Argentine look." The nightclubs of New York had heard about this tango man. Impresarios offered him a contract, without ever seeing Guillermo dance. All he had to do was sign. But he would not scribble his *G* for strangers. He wasn't really rich. But he bought a finca for his parents, who were stunned by his success at doing nothing but dance. An American movie star fell in love with him. Was it Ginger Rogers or Joan Blondell? Rafaela wasn't sure.

"Some people like to call him a maricon. 'El Matador

only loved boys.' But that is a lie. I met three or four women who slept with him. They are very, very old. They all said he was tremendo, a killer in bed."

Rafaela promised her a love story about this Guillermo who wore purple pants around all the Medellín princesses and the coffee merchants' wives. He wouldn't adopt the style of Buenos Aires or Bogotá. He didn't know the style of Buenos Aires. All he knew was his purple pants . . . and the orange hat he'd inherited from the slums around the old bus stations. This hat had a very high crown and an ostrich feather tucked under the silk ribbon. He wore it while he squatted over the toilet, dreaming of some tango step. Or when he was in the middle of a knife fight, because that cockatoo color never failed to distract his enemies.

And he liked to go courting in his orange hat. The richest widows chased El Matador, but he could never mingle love and money in his own mind. "He was a tango king, no?" said Rafaela. "He would not dance for total strangers or piss in the temple of love."

"Ah," Yolanda said. "All I hear is piss, piss, piss. Tell me about the chica, before I make in my pants."

"She was not a princess, not even a paisa."

"Then what was she, por favor?"

"A mulata from the Caribbean coast."

"A relative of yours, Rafaela?"

"No. We were not related. She worked at a hospedaje on the Avenida Sucre. But it was only temporary. She wanted to be an actress or a tango queen. But there were no tango queens in Medellín, and only one king."

"I see," said Yolanda, growing suspicious. "What was her name?"

"Tulipa Dawn."

Yolanda started to laugh, but she didn't want to hurt the pace of the story. "Tulipa Dawn. I see."

Guillermo began to haunt the bus stations, and that's how the rumors spread that he was a cabrón, looking to "buy" young gigolos at the back of a bus. But Guillermo had much more sentimental reasons for being there. He'd grown up near the terminals, and it comforted him to drink in the smell of gasoline and watch the pasajeros arrive with their little cardboard boxes, which held everything they had in the world. And he vowed to himself that when he died he would have no more possessions than could fit into a pasejero's box.

"But I want to know about Tulipa Dawn."

"Bruja," Rafaela said. "Don't hurry me. A story needs time."

It was while he was loitering at the terminals in his orange hat, with the brim pulled over one eye and the ostrich feather growing bald, that he first met Tulipa. She was coming off the Expreso from Cartagena, where she had been visiting the aunts who raised her. She was wearing sandals and an old yellow dress. She smiled at the beggars and gave them all the centavos she had in her purse. And it was this one simple gesture that destroyed the equilibrium of a tango king.

He followed her back to the hospedaje. It didn't disappoint him that she was a puta. Most of the women he'd been with were niñas of the street. He bargained with the Mamá Grande and bought Tulipa's services for the entire week.

"You know who I am?" he asked, shy in front of Tulipa.

"Sí. The tango king."

"And what if I arranged with the Mamá Grande to visit you on a permanent basis?"

"Whatever you like."

"Do you have other admirers?"

"Sí."

"Then you will have to dispossess yourself of them."

"I cannot."

"Why?" he asked, gloomy all of a sudden.

"Because I also see them on a permanent basis."

"Then we do not understand each other. Permanent does not mean other men."

He made love to Tulipa. It was violent, but also sweet. But she insisted on meeting her obligations to those other "permanentes." Guillermo toyed with the idea of killing them. But one was a police chief. Another was a judge. A third was a senator . . . and so on.

He danced at the rumbeaderos.

"Make her your partner, Guillermo," insisted one of his friends. "That's what she wants. If you dance with her, she will give up all her clients and you will be her caballero."

"Stupido," said the tango king. "I never sleep with my dancing partners. It would destroy the distance . . . and then there would be no electric line. I feel nothing for my partners."

"Is that your secret, El Matador?"

But the tango king could not talk to such a bobo. He returned to the hospedaje and offered to buy up Tulipa's contract.

"Maestro," said the Mamá Grande, "it will do no good. She is a costena. They are very stubborn people, the Caribes. Even if I sold her to you, Tulipa would not accept."

And so the tango king had to go on sharing Tulipa Dawn. She behaved like his mujer all the while she was with him. They would walk to the market together, sit in the movie houses, have long, elaborate meals at the Casa Caribe, where half the paisas of Medellín paid their respects to the tango king and "Dona Dawn."

Guillermo had already had six children by the time he was twenty-five. They lived with their mujeres, and if a mujer was scarce, Guillermo would hire an uncle or an aunt.

"Tulipa," he said. "I would like to have a child with you."

"Sí."

"But you will have to give up your clientele."

"Only while I am in labor."

"Then I will close the hospedaje and send your clients elsewhere."

"Sí. But they will follow you to your door."

And the tango king could no longer control his violence. He slapped his mujer. Her mouth started to bleed. He wiped her mouth with his shirt cuff, smiling a crazy smile.

"Would you like to dance with me, become my new partner?"

"Sí."

And he spent a month in retreat with his mujer, teaching her all the difficult passages of a tango king. And as her dancing deepened, Guillermo could feel his desire disappear. She no longer lived at the hospedaje. She had no clients. She is the only partner of El Matador whose name is still remembered, sometimes. He discarded her after five or six years. Her veins turned very blue from all the dancing. She bought a hospedaje of her own. Guillermo never saw her again.

12

THEY HAD a long cry over Tulipa Dawn, the mujer with the blue veins. It was then, Yolanda decided, after his desire was done, that Guillermo became such a big bandido, taxing the campesinos' milk and bread, while he gathered an army around him. That's what the loss of love can do to a man. It turns him into a politician. She didn't dare ask Rafaela to finish her tale, because then Yolanda would have had to reveal her own state secret about the death of the tango king. And she didn't want to spoil the romance that all the niñas had of Guillermo disappearing into the sky.

"Ah, los hombres," Yolanda said.

"Los hombres . . . they are such pathetic fish."

Yolanda didn't think about it much when Rafaela herself disappeared. She's gone on a pilgrimage to Cartagena, birthplace of Tulipa Dawn. That's what Yolanda figured until she realized that Rafaela's door had been sealed by the Securidad. No one tells me anything, she muttered to herself and took a colectivo down into the red and yellow lights of Little Manhattan. The driver discharged all his passengers at the

Parque Bolivar, and Yolanda walked to that bright red box of the Securidad. The iguanas winked at her.

"La novia," they said. "La novia del presidente."

Jacob's secretary tried to discourage Yolanda. "He is occupied with important matters, mamzelle."

"Then I'll wait."

The colonel arrived in half an hour, his jacket full of sweat. The scars had darkened around his eyes. He looked like a blind man. He invited Yolanda into his office.

"Why did you arrest Rafaela? Are you dissatisfied with the way she irons your dollar bills?"

"Don't mock me. You may have a letter from the White House, but this is Medellín. Letters get lost, and so do people . . . Rafaela is a spy. She works for Taita."

"All the niñas are rubenistas."

"I'm not talking about philosophy. We did not capture Ruben at your little palace, because he escaped through Rafaela's window. He planted her at the Suez."

"Where is she?"

"In my cellars, mamzelle."

"But she's your novia. You've had a child with Rafaela."

"And she takes advantage of that . . . I will not harm the child. But I cannot invite her onto my couch at the Securidad while she scratches little diagrams of this building for Ruben."

He dropped a crumpled piece of paper into her lap. Yolanda unfolded it. She saw a tiny plan of the Securidad station.

"We extracted it from one of Ruben's bombers. This is his favorite target, the Securidad . . . it was my own imbecility. Rafaela wanted to dance the tango with me down in the dungeons. I obliged. This used to be a rumbeadero. Guillermo danced here with his Tulipa. In my cellars, mamzelle. And if I hadn't found the diagram, little Rafaela might have carried the bomb. He is very convincing, Ruben. He charms priests and putas with his talk of the Green revolution. 'I make drugs to buy milk for the campesinos,' he says. 'I build villages for our Indian brothers, the Huitotos,' he says. 'I'm a Green. I want to save the forests,' he says. But it is all part of his coca strategy. Taita loves to market himself. Newspapers adore him all over the world. But I couldn't care less about his global image. I live in Medellín; Medellín is what I know. He has assassinated a thousand and ten people since he has come to power. Iguanas, rival traficantes, newspaper editors, politicians, campesinos. Whoever gets in the way, he punishes, he hurts. I'll show you some examples of his art."

The colonel took a stack of photographs off his desk. Yolanda saw mutilated women, children, and men. She stopped looking after the fifth or sixth photograph and started to cry, because she couldn't say what all the mutilation meant. It seemed to her without any motive. This wasn't crack or alcohol madness, or homicide on a Hundred and Twenty-ninth Street.

She'd strayed too far. She wasn't a Commando. And she wasn't a paisa. And she couldn't stop crying. "Colonel, how do I know that my cousin is the author of all this?"

"Mamzelle, I don't mount atrocity exhibitions."

He seized her by her twill shirt and led her through a narrow door in the rear wall of his room. She entered some kind of crazily cluttered emergency ward. There were beds and bottles of blood. Yolanda heard a constant moaning. She couldn't find one doctor in the ward. She saw bandaged men and boys. The colonel pushed her toward one of the beds. The man lying in it was a mestizo with a missing arm and leg. He had a cigarette stuck in his fierce, unhappy face.

"Alejandro," Jacob said, "tell the señorita who it is that has harmed you."

"Taita."

"How?"

"With a bomba," said the mestizo.

"And why?"

"Because I didn't want to work anymore in his bomb brigade . . . I did not want to be the maker of orphans, señor colonel."

The colonel tugged at Yolanda. "Should I give you a tour of our little hospital at the Securidad?"

"No," she said.

They returned to his room.

"I have to have my own hospital. Ruben would murder these men . . . go back to Candelaria. I have declared a little bit of a general amnesty for your sake."

She wouldn't ride in the colonel's truck. She found a colectivo and rode up into the hills. There were four men in the collectivo, four men and a goat. The goat was terribly spoiled and sat on everybody's lap, including Yolanda's. The four men were farmers who'd been sacrificed to the civil war. The iguanas and Ruben's people kept trampling their crops. They would become marimberos, growers of marijuana rather than corn. It was the only crop that was respected in a civil war.

Yolanda got out of the colectivo and climbed up the stairs

of her hospedaje. Rafaela's door was open. She stood near the window, ironing deutsche marks and dollar bills. Yolanda could almost have believed that she'd never been gone. But she had cigarette burns on her wrists. And she'd grown less plump in the cellars of the Securidad.

"Bruja," she said, "don't ask me questions, please."

And then she volunteered to talk. "He loves me, that prick of a colonel. But he is a paisa. One of those secret Jews that Medellín is famous for."

"He swears he's not a clandestino."

"They all like to deny it. They worry about pogroms. They think the other criollos will rise up against them and rob them of their land and their lives. So they marry their own daughters and breed little lunatics."

"The colonel married his daughter. I can't believe it."

"Ah, bruja, you know what I mean. They marry each other and make children with mulatas like me. But don't let him fool you. I have seen hebreo symbols in his office."

"What symbols, Rafaela?"

"Symbols, that's all. Little things, like a rabino's red hat."

"There are mucho rabinos in Manhattan. But they do not wear red hats. Red is a cardinal's color."

"Sí. That's why the clandestinos have adopted it. It's much safer for their rabinos to wear red."

"But I have never met such a rabino in Medellín."

"They wouldn't reveal themselves to a stranger."

"And you have met them?" Yolanda asked.

"Many times."

"Then take me to one."

"Bruja, I cannot be indiscreet."

And Rafaela returned to her ironing board.

13

I T WAS just Yolanda's luck that her only friend in Candelaria was a girl who talked riddles most of the time. But it was better than eating banana splits on her own. They would stroll Candle Street together, Yolanda wearing a bright red dress she'd bought at the dollaria, because the other stores had run out of goods. And with Rafaela to guide her Yolanda didn't feel like such an outcast. Medellín itself was no longer a maze. She could enter into the fabric of the city as long as Rafaela was around.

They would eat at little black market restaurants, which only served invited guests, and Yolanda drank such soups that one could only dream of, with chicken, corn, and brown sugar that had been passed over a flame. And the two chicas would pay for their meals in dollars or deutsche marks (credit cards and bank checks were unknown currencies in the barrios of Medellín).

They would walk arm in arm, like a pair of sisters, while jíbaros in the street serenaded them with filthy songs. The red roofs seemed to burn over Yolanda's eyes. The sun sat on her shoulder. It was Navidad in Candelaria, without red and yellow lights, but Navidad nonetheless. I could live here, Yolanda thought to herself. I could survive on a ration of banana splits with my girlfriend Rafaela. But she was only living on a Commando's borrowed time. Sooner or later she'd have to hold herself accountable to the president of the United States.

It was during one of her walks with Rafaela, while the bombs popped, that a jeep appeared on Candle Street, which was forbidden by law. But this jeep belonged to the Securidad. It was bright red, and looked like rumbeadero furniture. Colonel Jacob sat in the driver's seat. He was all alone. He didn't have one bodyguard in a black beret.

"Chicas," he cooed with a twist of his head. "Get in."

The two girls climbed into the jeep, with Rafaela almost in the colonel's lap. All of Rafaela's stories suddenly made sense, because the colonel was like a lovesick cavalier. He wore the silk scarf of a tango king. He didn't take his two girls into the heart of Medellín, where the bombers were. He went higher in the hills, one arm around Rafaela's waist. He would have made a perfect target. But this was Candelaria. And the rubenistas wouldn't have bombed their own barrio.

They arrived at a finca that was both glorious and a little rundown. There were orchids all over the place, such flowers as Yolanda had never seen in all the barrios of her life—with leaves that were a dark mosaic, and petals that could have been ripe fruit. But the garden was full of potholes, and the house had a meandering roof that seemed ready to cave in. Yolanda, who wasn't religious, crossed herself as she entered with Rafaela and the colonel.

There was nothing elaborate inside. Rooms with simple tables and chairs. A woman sat at one of the tables, sipping from a Coca Cola Grande with the help of a colored straw. She was wearing an old shawl, and Yolanda could tell that she was blind. Her eyes registered nothing when the colonel approached. He whispered in her ear.

"Ah," the woman said, "una turista."

"No, mama," the colonel said. "A brave soldier from the barrios of New York."

"Ah," she said, "los norteamericanos have mujeres in their army."

"Sí. But this is a special case. She is with the environmental commandos."

The blind woman laughed. "We also have such commandos. But when they try to punish the gold miners for poisoning our rivers, they shoot their own foot."

"But that is because the minister who trains them is a fool and a thief, like most of our ministers, and receives a profit from the miners. But I did not come here to argue, mama. The young lady is an admirer of yours."

"Colonel," the blind woman said. "I am not dressed to meet admirers. You should have called on the telefono."

"You never answer the telefono. So it would have been futile."

"But at least it would have been polite."

"Que putería," the colonel said, "you are much too clever for a policeman of the Securidad." And then he turned to Yolanda. "Bruja, come here and say hello to Dona Tulipa Dawn."

And Yolanda nearly wet her pants, because it was like touching history to be that close to Guillermo Gaudí's tango partner and lost love. She never would have guessed that Tulipa was still alive.

"Niña," the blind woman said, "let me hold your face."

Yolanda was confused. No one had ever made a request like that. And the colonel had to shove her down into Tulipa's lap. The blind woman had the softest hands in the world.

"She is a guapa, colonel, this Commando of yours."

"But no more beautiful than Tulipa Dawn," the colonel said.

"Ah, you love to flatter. But I was not beautiful. Only handsome, a little."

"You were the greatest beauty of your time. Everyone says so."

"But you were not there. The paisas, I admit, are not very handsome. But there were mulatas in the hotels of Maracaibo Street who would have stopped your heart. Guillermo happened to notice me coming off a bus. He was a bobo. He fell in love. But if he had seen those other niñas . . ."

"It would have made no difference, mama."

"Perhaps. Love is a monstrous thing. It is not worth two centavos . . . what is the little Commando's name?"

"Yolanda Ramirez," the colonel said.

"You brought her to my finca and she asks no questions. A very curious girl."

"She is stunned by your presence," the colonel said, nudging Yolanda and whispering. "Bruja, you are embarrassing us . . . ask her a question."

"I don't know what to say."

Rafaela and the colonel pinched her arm.

"Ask."

"Dona Tulipa, what was it like to be the mujer of a tango king?"

"Before I danced with the bobo or while I danced with him?"

"Both," Yolanda said.

"Ah," Tulipa said. "Colonel, you made a good selection. I like this girl. She knows how to wound in a delicate way . . . Yolanda, he was like most paisas, rich or poor. Violent and very lazy. And a better lover when he danced."

"Forgive me," Yolanda said. "But I thought he wouldn't make love after you became his tango partner."

"He was impotente, sí. But not on a wooden floor. I always had a climax during the dance. You could not imagine the pleasure. So many people watching us. And Guillermo with a look of murder in his eyes. I had all the satisfaction a mujer could want."

"And when he discarded you?"

"It was his own fear. He could not live with the thought that I took more from the dancing than he ever did."

"Did you ever dance again?"

"No. It would have been a foolishness without Guillermo. I had other lovers, better than a tango king. But it had no echo outside the bed. I was his mujer, even after he became invisible to me. I suffered. I was alone. But I always had the memory of his dance. Ask the colonel. He will tell you. In Medellín the tango is a matter of life and death. The paisas have produced nothing, nothing but this crazy dance."

The blind woman fell asleep. Rafaela kissed her hand. The colonel shoved the two girls out of the finca.

SISTER OF MERCY

14

SHE WAS like a dreamer in Jacob's jeep, trying to absorb what Tulipa Dawn had said. She had a thousand other questions for the blind woman, and they'd all go unasked, because Yolanda had always been a little tongue-heavy, even when she was a child, playing doctor with Ruben Falcone. And she wondered if all that furtive play under the stairs was like an invitation to a dance, her own sort of tango.

Rafaela lay against the colonel's shoulder as he drove down from the finca. And Yolanda had to wonder about this romance, because it was like Guillermo and Tulipa all over again, even if Jacob wasn't a tango king. The wings of his white scarf flew around his shoulders. He kissed Rafaela and seemed to steer with the back of his head. And perhaps the story of Guillermo and Tulipa was the story of Medellín itself, with the paisas and their mulata sweethearts whom they would never marry.

The colonel didn't take them back to Candle Street. He brought them to a neighborhood of rumbeaderos in Guillermo's part of town, the barrios south of a business district that was always being bombed. Ruben had closed the stock exchange, and the traders had never bothered to reopen with such banditos around. And so there was a pall over the district, even with its red and yellow lights of Navidad. Each avenue had its quota of checkpoints, but no one bothered this colonel of the Securidad. The streets were filled with "los hijos de la miseria," the homeless children of Medellín who moved in packs. They carried sticks and cursed at passing cars. No orphanage could hold them. The "chinos" had gone wild.

Iguanas had to fire their guns at these wild gangs, but the guns were of little use, because the chinos had learned how to dodge a bullet. They were kept out of Little Manhattan by a brigade of special troops, but they wandered in their wolf packs throughout the barrios.

Yolanda looked at their faces from the heights of the jeep. They had such bitterness in their dark eyes, that Yolanda wanted to get out of the jeep and herd them home with her to the Suez.

"Colonel, can't you do something about the chinos?"

"No, mamzelle. I have tried. But I would require an army to meet their army, and I would never win. I have appealed to the minister of education. Each year he has his 'operaciones de limpieza' to clear the streets. But where should we put the chinos? In a concentration camp? Don't worry. They become rubenistas after a while. They run drugs for the traficantes."

"That is not an answer," Yolanda said.

"I'm afraid in Medellín it is."

And they entered the Rumbeadero de la Paz on one of

Medellín's mean streets, but not until the colonel had ra-
dioed one of his soldiers to babysit for the jeep. The chinos
would have dismantled it in five minutes if the red jeep
didn't have a bodyguard.

Yolanda wasn't in the mood to dance. This rumbeadero
didn't have any of Ruben's doubles. It was filled with igua-
nas, clerks from the local Ministry of Justice, captains of
the Securidad, and their afternoon brides—"tintas" who'd
presented them with a whole brood of illegitimate chil-
dren—all of them dancing the tango to an orchestra of
middle-aged men in spangled blue coats. The orchestra was
a relic from Guillermo's time, and might have been a relic
even then, because the tango was old-fashioned from the
day it was born, at least the tango medellín. The dancers
never looked at each other. They moved with the precision
of dreamwalkers, every dancer caught in the blindness of his
or her own dream. And that must have been Guillermo's
genius. He was the ultimate dreamwalker, acting out that
long sleep of Medellín with the languid violence of his
gestures. He took the Medellínos into the furthest point of
sleep.

And when Yolanda saw the colonel dance in his white
scarf, she realized that the whole crazy town had become
Guillermo's ghost. All the paisas needed that oblivion of the
dance.

One of the captains paused in front of Yolanda.

"May I have the pleasure, mamzelle?"

And before she could say no, no, she had a limp, a belly-
ache, menstrual cramps, high blood pressure, weakened
lungs, a damaged heart, and a whole tattoo of illnesses, he
seized her by the hand and led her onto that floor of tango

dancers. She was mortified. She didn't fit into this mad scheme. She wasn't a paisa or a mulata from the coast. She had no business dancing here. And then she closed her eyes, ignored her partner's grip, and fell into the dream of Guillermo Gaudí.

But it didn't last. Just as she was becoming a tango artist, she heard a very strange crump, as if the floor had split. Yolanda tumbled into some tango king. The teardrops of a chandelier socked her shoulder. She started to scream. She was lying among women who looked like rag dolls. The men had blood in their eyes.

She awoke in a ward that was a little too familiar. She was lying in a bed at the Securidad, in the colonel's hospital room. The patients around her were fallen commandos, like herself, casualties of the explosion at the Rumbeadero de la Paz. My first bombing, Yolanda muttered like a crazy woman. It's true that her head wasn't clear. She'd never learn the tango medellín no matter how long she remained here. She was doomed to live outside the city's own secrets. She was just another gringa on some sort of mission to Medellín. She fell into a terrific gloom.

And that's when she noticed the unmistakable green eyes of Muzo Martinez, acting minister of justice and chief of the Colombian Air Force. The comandante wore battle fatigues. He had a pair of pistols to go with his two watches. His field jacket was a garden of hand grenades.

"General," she said, "I always meant to ask why you wear two watches."

"A habit I picked up on the streets of Medellín when I was a homeless one."

"You were one of the chinos?"

"Sí. I had my own gallada, my own gang. And to wear two watches, señorita, was enough status to last for a lifetime. I learned all my politics as a chino de la calle. I did my military training with the gallada."

"And how did you graduate?"

"By having a successful gang. I didn't die in a traffic accident, like some of the niños. I didn't starve. I raised five brothers and sisters in the streets. And then I allowed a padre to discover me . . . I needed a sponsor, no? I taught myself to read and write. I was the most successful chino in the history of Medellín. Journalists came from Madrid to interview me. El niño fabuloso. I sang on the television. I could have had a career in broadcasting. But I became a cop. It suited my temperament. And then I moved into the air force. It was my passion to fly a plane. And now I am what I am."

"Then why don't you do something about the niños?"

"Yes, I know. El gaminismo colombiano. The whole world talks about it, like it talks about Taita, the Green traficante . . . I no longer allow the journalists to come. It is our story, not an international freak show."

"But what will you do?"

"Nothing. El gaminismo is a training ground for soldiers. The strong will survive. And how can I help the weak? Half of them are bobos. They would die in an institution."

"But you could educate them, send them to school."

"Ah, yes. That is the North American way. We do not have

the money or the time, even with the new Marshall Plan from your presidente. The money goes into all the cracks. Ruben is still alive and the chinos will never go away . . . ah, but we did save you from the rubenistas and their bomb. It was a very big one."

"How many people died?"

"Six. Seven. I am not sure."

"And my friend Rafaela?"

"Ah, you mean the tinta that Colonel Jacob is crazy about. I haven't seen her on the casualty list."

"But where is she?"

"I cannot account for everyone. I'm a busy man."

And he went into his hand-kissing routine, bowing in front of Yolanda's bed with that garden of hand grenades.

"I think we will be sending you home. Ruben cannot be such a close cousin if he tried to kill you. So what is the point of having you here? Shall we trail you like dogs until the next bombing. No. The time has passed for a truce. We will get him out of the country, but in a wooden box. Then all the journalists can sing a Mass for the Green traficante . . . my men will come for you tomorrow when you are feeling a little better."

"Where's Professor Sparks?"

"In the Amazon, chasing gold miners. He thinks he's Don Quixote . . . Ruben is also in the Amazon, hiding in a finca. He will not live very long, I promise. I don't care how many Green congressmen start to cry. They can have their rain forest when that piece of shit paisa is mine."

"Ruben was born in New York City."

"He's still a paisa," said the comandante, kissing her hand for the last time. And what could Yolanda read in that dark face with the green eyes? One more ex–chino de la calle who happened to be minister of justice and marshal of the air force.

Yolanda fell into a dream. She was dancing with Guillermo. The eyes of the whole rumbeadero were upon her and the king. But the problem was that *this* Guillermo, whoever he was, didn't have a face, just a head without hair or the hurly-burly of a single feature. Yet she moved with all the staccato grace of Guillermo's queen. Her line followed his. Guillermo didn't need a face. Yolanda had such an orgasm as she'd never had with one of her bank robber boyfriends.

Then there was a face in front of her eyes. Colonel Jacob had come for a visit. His right arm sat in a sling. Yolanda had a curious feeling that this Securidad station was no longer his.

"Muzo has declared martial law," he said.

"Where's Rafaela?"

"Muerta," he said. "She died in my arms . . . I will not recover so fast, mamzelle."

He sat down on Yolanda's bed, took his arm out of the sling, and held Yolanda's hand.

The colonel visited her again, brought Yolanda some soup.

"I cannot forgive myself . . . but if I hadn't arrested her, she would have fallen into the hands of Muzo's commandos de la muerte."

"Muzo has his own death squads?"

"He isn't the only one, mamzelle. Every comandante has a death list. The rubenistas have their lists too. That's how things are done in Medellín. It's a town of tango dancers and commandos de la muerte . . . but Ruben wouldn't have bombed a rumbeadero. That was Muzo's work. Now he has martial law. He will choke the rubenistas to death. He has already shut the rumbeaderos. And he has taken down the Sinfonía de Luces. We will have a very mournful Navidad this year. Hombres will have to think twice about dressing up like Don Ruben. Muzo has give orders to shoot all the doubles on sight."

"And you?" Yolanda asked.

"Ah, I am under house arrest. But it is nothing, mamzelle. Muzo has done this before. He doesn't trust the paisas. But he cannot rule Medellín without us. So I will work on my memoirs. And I will take a holiday from being a policeman. It won't last."

"I'm also his prisoner," Yolanda said. "Muzo wants me out of the country by tomorrow."

"Of course. You cannot deliver Ruben. And you might become an embarrassment for him with your letter from the White House."

"I'm not going," she said.

"Mamzelle, it's martial law and this is Medellín. People disappear, even novias del presidente."

"I'm not going."

"Then I will have to put you under house arrest."

"You can't. I'm Muzo's prisoner, not yours."

"I still have limited powers," the colonel said, taking his arm out of the sling again. But he couldn't stop grieving. Yolanda and the colonel cried in each other's arms.

"Rafaela," they said, while all the other wounded watched.

There was bedlam at the Securidad. Soldiers moved at a furious pace, but there was no one to govern while the colonel was under house arrest. Muzo's men fought with the regulars of the Securidad. They couldn't seem to find a password that would unite them into a functioning army. They bumped each other in the halls. Corporals would spit at captains and lieutenant colonels. Sergeants would rule a particular floor. And it was in this little hurricane that Yolanda got out of bed, looked at her bruises, got dressed, and marched out of the Securidad, saluting generals and privates who figured she was one more of Muzo's mistresses. Why else would a mujer be so brazen in the middle of martial law?

She crossed Junin Street and walked south, toward that barrio of rumbeaderos where Guillermo had danced. Jacob hadn't lied. All the Christmas lights were gone from Medellín. It was la ciudad dolorosa, the town that couldn't even mourn itself. La violencia had overwhelmed Medellín. It was prey to whoever could hold it—general or traficante—and no hombre could hold it very long. And it tumbled into a kind of anarchy, even with Muzo's martial law.

It was the chinos who benefited most. Their galladas occupied more and more of the city. They would plunder a store and return to their alleys. Iguanas would shoot at them "wholesale," but the chinos didn't seem to care what casualties they sustained. Life and death were cheap in la ciudad dolorosa. The children might lose half a gallada in a single foray, and then regroup into yet another wolf pack.

Jacob might have been able to prevent some of the slaughter. He'd involved himself with the children. He'd arrested them, harangued them, delivered food to their hideaways, and they loved to see him dance at the rumbeaderos, because he moved like a chino, with a violence that was loving *and* indifferent at the same time. But the colonel was under house arrest. And the children weren't so fond of Muzo, who'd grown up in *their* barrios, who'd been a chino de la calle, like themselves. They thought of him as a detested older brother, a chino who had survived the streets and had formed his own great gallada to hunt them down. They would have picked the eyes out of his head, as Muzo's commandos de la muerte often did to them.

Not all the children were warriors. There were locos and little girls who had to distance themselves from the clashes. They starved unless they had an older brother. And sometimes there were galladas of little girls who scavenged as much as they could. They had to protect themselves from kidnappers who might herd them into prostitution rings and often were soldiers themselves. So these galladas carried razor blades and sharpened bottle caps and stones. And when Yolanda saw one such gallada, her heart began to squeeze, because nothing in Nueva York was like this. The little girls had never washed. They wore the rottenest rags. They had no shoes. Their eyes were caked with dirt. Yolanda would either have to help or run back screaming to the Securidad.

"Como se llama, como se llama?" she kept asking the girls.

They danced away from Yolanda, giving their names like a gang of coquettes. Estela. Marina. Charo. Immaculata. Rosa. Rosa Secunda. Gabriela. Rosa Trez. And some of them had animal names, like Cugara and Tigra. Others had no names at all, and existed at the very edge of the gallada.

Yolanda followed the girls deeper and deeper into the barrio. She had no money to give them. Someone had stolen her chastity belt while she lay unconscious at the Securidad. And so she was some sister of mercy who couldn't even feed a child. One of the chicas had to offer her a hard-boiled egg, or Yolanda might have starved. The egg was dirty. Yolanda wiped it against her own skin.

She'd become a mascot to this gallada, a sainted fool who followed children around. No one scratched her face. She was called La Sardina, the stupid one. And whenever there was food to roast at a back-alley bonfire, Yolanda tasted it first, like the gallada's own witch.

But this idyll didn't last very long. A gang of wild boys stumbled upon the bonfire, stole all the food, punched the little girls, and kidnapped Yolanda. They bound her hands with wire, they poked under her dress, squeezed her nipples, touched her while she was lying on the ground.

Their leader called himself Rudolfo. He was either six or seven. He took the most pleasure squeezing Yolanda's nipples, or disappearing inside her dress. He would root with his head and leave horrible marks on Yolanda's thighs.

"Who are you, mammy, and answer quick."

"Yolanda Ramirez of the Christian Commandos."

"Los commandos de la muerte?"

"No," she said.

"Sí. You're Muzo's puta. He bites you between the legs."

And these wild boys tore at Yolanda, kissing her, biting her, until she rolled on the ground like a lunatic. Santa Maria, she would never survive the city of Medellín. The piranhas ate at her flesh, and as she swooned Yolanda heard a voice.

"Coño, get away from that girl."

"Pappy, don't interfere," Rudolfo said, continuing to bite Yolanda.

She could feel someone picking the piranhas off her body. She'd recognized that voice. It belonged to her little cousin, Ruben the traficante. Yolanda blinked. Ruben was lying in a wheelbarrow. A whole other gang of chinos was wheeling him around. He slapped at Rudolfo.

"Go on, give her some water."

"I thought you were at your finca in the Amazon," Yolanda said.

"I never left Medellín."

He had bandages on both his legs.

"I was at the rumbeadero when you arrived with Colonel Jacob."

"You crazy," she said, "it was filled with iguanas."

"None of the iguanas recognized me . . . little sister, I love to dance."

LA FINCA DOLORES

15

HE WAS better than a tango king, this paisa Robin Hood, Ruben Falcone, born on a Hundred and Twenty-ninth Street in the Latino fields of New York City. The chinos de la calle had taken a wounded man and found him a wheelbarrow when his own caballeros couldn't get through General Muzo's checkpoints. He was stranded in this city of sadness, attended to by an army of children. The children had their own king, Rudolfo, who was as much a guerrilla as any of the activist priests. At six he already had a philosophy. To grab and run, grab and run, until the iguanas got tired. He was a thinker at seven. He would have to join Muzo before he was eleven or twelve, because Muzo had the guns and the ammunition. But Ruben was a much better ally right now. Ruben had the coca and the niñas, deutsche marks and dollar bills. And Ruben was a bandido, like the chinos themselves.

And so the king could tolerate an occasional cuff on the head from Taita, who filled his pockets with deutsche marks and was the number one traficante in the world. Taita was also a "verde," but the king didn't understand all this talk about green planets. The Orinoco didn't run through Medellín, and there were no crocodiles on the Avenida Bolivar. He'd heard about Taita's plantation in the swamps, which had its own airport and ice cream factory and mujeres with big nanas, like this Dona Yolanda that Ruben had stolen from him. Sí, the mujer looked a little like a cow, but that did not bother the king. He would have bitten all her blood if Ruben hadn't stopped him.

And so they sat at the fire, Ruben, the mujer, Rudolfo, and Rudolfo's lieutenants, and they toasted marshmallows they'd swiped from the Securidad and its commissary on the Avenida Sucre. It was Rudolfo who'd washed Ruben's legs and bought a cream from the brujo on Calle 23 to heal the wounds. And Rudolfo had to pay a hundred deutsche marks for the wheelbarrow. A horse and sled would have been too obvious. And how could you hide a horse? But a wheelbarrow was the best transportation in town when you lived in the alleys.

"Taita," the boy said, "you owe me a billion for the wheelbarrow. But lend me the mujer. I want to give her another feel."

"Shut up."

"Who went to the witch doctor and got you the magic salve? I saved your legs."

"What can I do about it?"

"Sell me the mujer."

"Bobo, she's my fiancée."

The king looked at one and then the other. He wasn't in the mood to roast marshmallows with a mujer whose nanas he couldn't bite. "You never mentioned her, pappy."

"That's because she has been living in the North. We have been engaged for twenty years. Ask her yourself."

"I never talk to mujeres. It's like talking to a cow."

Yolanda got up from that bonfire and began hurling marshmallows at the little king, who took it as a sign of real significance that he'd made the mujer angry. And Ruben had to navigate on his own inside the wheelbarrow to restrain her. He whispered in Yolanda's ear.

"He was born in the streets. He's a little wild. He never knew his mother and father."

"I don't care."

"Humor him, little sister. The bastard has kept me alive."

Yolanda bent over the king, picked him up, cradled him between her breasts before he could start to struggle. He'd never been held by a mujer like that, against her nanas. He took in her smell. It was more powerful than coca leaves or a stick of bareto. She rocked him for a minute and then returned him to his place at the head of the bonfire. The king was in heaven. Then he saw the zambo standing over the fire, warming his hands a week before Christmas.

"Who invited him, pappy?"

"Shut up."

"The boy's right," Yolanda said. "He's Muzo's assassin. He would have killed you if he could."

"Yes and no," Ruben said from his wheelbarrow. Then he turned to the king. "Coño, be polite. Offer the man a marshmallow."

"I don't eat with zambos," the boy said. "That's my law."

"Do I have to get up from the barrow and feed him myself?"

The little king roasted a marshmallow for ChiChi, who saved it and sat next to the wheelbarrow.

"What are our prospects?" Ruben asked.

"Not too good."

"But if Muzo thinks I'm in the Amazon, he shouldn't be on guard."

"Ruben, please. I planted the bomb at the rumbeadero. Muzo knows where you are. That's why he has all the checkpoints."

"Ah, that was your bomb."

"Pappy, should we kill him?" the king asked.

"No. He was doing his job. That's the life of a double agent."

"Then at least let me take out his eyes with a marshmallow stick," said Yolanda. "My friend Rafaela died at the rumbeadero because of him."

"Mamzelle," the zambo said. "It was the smallest bomb I knew how to make . . . what could I have said to Muzo if there had been no casualties?"

"I still think you ought to die."

"Shhh," Ruben said. "ChiChi, I can't sit forever in a wheelbarrow. The iguanas are bound to find me. You'll have to smuggle me through the lines . . . with my fiancée."

"That's twice the danger, Don Ruben. I wasn't considering a second party."

"You'll be paid," Ruben said.

"That is not the point."

"You'll be paid."

Ruben glanced at the king, who roasted another marshmallow for Muzo's favorite assassin.

They didn't dare travel at night, according to the zambo, who had all of Muzo's strategies in his head. The general had killed the Christmas lights in downtown Medellín because he didn't want Taita to escape in a confusion of red and yellow bulbs strung across the streets. He had enormous searchlights stationed at the mouth of each alley. And the zambo couldn't move Taita while those searchlights played in the dark. Taita's shadow would have hovered over the alley walls like the wings of a giant bat.

And so the boys picked him out of the wheelbarrow and he slept beside Yolanda on the alley floor. It was an odd sensation, the memory of her flesh as a little girl, his sweetheart from Madison and a Hundred and Twenty-ninth. Why should it have troubled him so? The paisa Robin Hood was a billionaire. He had bank accounts in nineteen countries. He could have built a rumbeadero inside a Swiss chalet and danced his brains out, but he would have been bored within a week. The tango medellín was meaningless in a Swiss chalet.

"Yolanda," he said, nudging her while the little king and his gallada stood watch and ChiChi stoked the fire. "Yolanda, do you still have the ring I gave you?"

"Crazyhead, that was twenty years ago . . . a tin ring. I wore it out waiting for you. Tin expands in the heat. It broke and I kept fixing it with Band-Aids."

"But do you still have it?"

"Sí," she said, snuggling next to him. "Now let me sleep."

"I don't believe you."

"Bobo, I lent it to my little son. He wears it on his wrist. I was a convict. I couldn't take all my belongings to jail . . . and if you're so concerned, why didn't you write to me once in those twenty years? Or make a phone call? You have the deutsche marks."

"I was busy," Ruben said.

"Yeah, buying and selling fincas . . . and handling cocaine."

"And becoming a Green, don't forget."

"You can't fool me, little cousin . . . I'm as much a Green as you are. And I've never been near a rain forest. You can't fool me."

She turned her back on Ruben and deliberately started to snore.

"Wait until you get to the Finca Dolores," he said, but the little sister was fast asleep.

16

THEY ALMOST didn't make it.

ChiChi couldn't camouflage a wheelbarrow and make it through the general's lines. Muzo's death squads were all over the place. They shot children and old ladies, anyone who looked like a rubenista. So ChiChi commandeered an ambulance that belonged to the Securidad. This ambulance had also served as a torture chamber. It was cluttered with hot wires and medieval contraptions only the paisas would have used, pulleys and neck locks that dated from the Inquisition.

Ruben was loaded onto the ambulance without his wheelbarrow.

"ChiChi, I've grown fond of that thing. It's almost part of my skin."

"Then learn to get along without it. I'm not traveling with a wheelbarrow."

He climbed aboard with Yolanda. The little king looked at them forlornly from the ground. He started to sniffle in front of his own gallada.

"Pappy, take me too."

"Can't," Ruben said, without looking into the king's eyes.

"Pappy, I'll never get to see the Finca Dolores."

"You will. Another time."

"Pappy, there is no other time."

"What about your troops?"

"They're chinos. They'll find a different king . . . take me."

"Puta de merde," ChiChi said. "That's the limit."

"ChiChi," Ruben said. "He's seven. Barely a boy."

"Barely a boy, eh? He's on Muzo's death list, right under your name. Rudolfo, el rey de los chinos. He's murdered, sodomized men and women."

"Nothing you and I haven't done."

Yolanda stared at Rudolfo and started to cry. The little king had bitten her to pieces—her nipples were still raw—but she couldn't help feeling sorry for him. He was another lost boy, like her Benjamin. She reached down and swept him up onto the ambulance. And the zambo didn't say a word. He covered Ruben and Yolanda and the boy with a tarpaulin and drove the ambulance across the alleys. He had no fixed route. He let the siren wail. He bumped into walls. The commandos de la muerte got out of his way, recognizing him as one of their own. But the iguanas who occupied the checkpoints wanted to know what he was doing with a Securidad bus. Twice they tried to storm the ambulance and twice he had to say, "This is General Muzo's business, señors."

"Ah, the torture bus."

"Sí."

"But let us have a little look."

"Hermanos, you don't want to look."

He could have killed the checkpoint soldiers, of course. But he didn't want a little war on the way out of Medellín, because Muzo would have sniffed that trail of blood. So ChiChi had to play himself, the zambo who was half human, Muzo's pet snake. He rattled his head, he foamed a little at the mouth, and drove Ruben to a barn twenty klicks south of the city.

"Ruben," he said, "I think I shit my pants."

"It won't be the first time, or the last."

The zambo removed the tarpaulin and kissed Ruben, Yolanda, and the little killer king, and waited for the rubenistas to arrive. Two men emerged from the fields behind the barn like large mice. They were part of Ruben's Indian cadre. They wouldn't speak Spanish, but they could fly a plane. They frightened the zambo who also had Ticuna blood, but couldn't compete with them in any language. They were hunters, not assassins, fishermen, and fliers of planes. They were known as the birdmen, because sometimes they wore wings made of condor feathers and a special wax, and they would flap around in the rain forest, float among the trees, wearing primitive paint and smoking black cigars. They frightened all the animals for miles. But they wouldn't wear wings this close to Medellín.

They opened the barn, waltzed a biplane out of it that was part paper, part metal, part wood. It looked like a dangerous toy. They fiddled with the prop, put on their own primitive aviator caps, stood on the bottom set of wings, patching the struts with some kind of staple gun, and only after that did they decide to approach the bus. They helped the three passengers down, one at a time, and insisted on carrying them to the biplane. Ruben didn't argue once. These were his Ticunas. The one who carried Yolanda smelled like rotting oranges. He smoked a very short cigar. He danced on the balls of his feet, and Yolanda felt as if she were about to fly. She couldn't understand why he hadn't burned his lips with such a short cigar.

Yolanda had never been inside such a maddening plane. It was like flying into the weather. The clouds filtered through the wings and collected at her feet. The birdmen had goggles. They could see in this atmosphere and guide the plane with their hands and feet. But Yolanda had to sit in all that soup. She was terrified. Not the little king, who drowned himself in the soup and tried to bite whatever he could. "Miracle," he said. "Pappy, I'm next to God." But pappy was asleep. He snored right through the plane's dips and stutters and all the shiverings of the wings.

Yolanda was convinced that at least one of the wings would fall off. They were held together with the birdmen's staples and seemed to bend against the sky. Bits of the paper tore in the wind and Yolanda could see the skeleton struts. And then one of the birdmen would climb out and repaper the wing.

She began to hunger for the ground of Medellín, for the safety of a banana split. Suddenly the sky fell and Yolanda could see the brown fingers of a river and the smokey green light of the rain forest. The ground glowed like pieces of phosphorus. The grass turned blue under Yolanda's scrutiny. It was like having your own kaleidoscope. Yolanda could manufacture color with her eyes.

Slowly, slowly, under the stuttering engine, Yolanda began to hear all the birds cry. It was like a soft, incessant wind, something that had entered her mind and would never leave. Now she understood the preachings of Professor Sparks. There was nothing like that wind in all the barrios she'd ever known. She'd been to the Bronx Zoo, she'd had her training as a Christian Commando in tidewater brack, but there wasn't that constant wind, which sang to Yolanda the song of her very own life, and was like a little civilization she didn't have to share.

A bald patch appeared in the jungle, like a crazy carpet. And the plane dove into that patch, and Yolanda was on the ground again, in Ruben's private airport. It wasn't grass or earth or anything monsters could have made. It was a gigantic strip of rubber the Ticunas had painted green. Other birdmen stood on this carpet. And even while the plane landed, the birdmen began to roll the carpet right off the face of the jungle. There were bits of shrubbery underneath, low-lying plants, like a little savannah the birdmen had sculpted with their own hands.

They carried Ruben off the plane, treated him like some kind of noisy child. These birdmen had painted their faces blue-black. It was magnificent camouflage, because the earth of the forest was that same color. The Ticunas weren't nasty, but they wouldn't talk to Yolanda or the little king, who were like baggage that Ruben had brought back from the land of sad people, which was Medellín in their vocabulary.

They picked up the plane and carried it into the jungle with them until there wasn't a trace of Ruben's airport. These birdmen were a tribe of brujos. Reality was only what their fingers told them. They could make and unmake. That was their particular music.

Mosquitoes as big as bats slapped at the birdmen, who grunted and returned the slaps. The little king copied these moves, grunting and socking with both fists. Yolanda stood in the wake of the birdmen. The mosquitoes left her alone.

They arrived at a jungle house that had no clearing or little garden or mound to plant a flagpole. It simply appeared. If Yolanda had walked two steps to the right she would have missed the house. The birdmen had built it, but the house had no history. And Yolanda understood right away that the Finca Dolores was one more piece of forest furniture. The birdmen could dismantle the finca and carry it on their backs. That was Ruben's strength. If Muzo's commandos came within a hundred miles, Ruben ran off with his Dolores.

Yolanda was startled by all the industry inside. It was packed with Ticunas and guerrilla priests and mujeres with bare breasts and technicians and clerks. It was as if Noah had filled his ark with humans instead of animals, and the ark had to pick itself up and float across a forest with the help of an Indian tribe. That was the Finca Dolores.

It had a movie theater, laboratories, a library, a puteadero, an arsenal, a health clinic, and an ice cream factory. The Ticunas adored ice cream. They invented new flavors out of jungle juices and the sweet bark of certain trees, but they were just as crazy about chocolate or vanilla, as crazy as a city girl or a chino de la calle would have been.

The finca had its own generators and water pumps and gasoline and spare propellers for the plane. The birdmen oiled these props night and day. Their doctors took care of

Ruben, putting leaves on his burns, feeding him flavors of ice cream that would drive his temperature down. They had him walking with a cane after a week. And even while he lay in bed he supervised all this industry. His accountant had a computer that could fit inside a hand, and the computer had enough memory to invent a new Amazon, but it couldn't pinpoint a problem the way Taita could or recognize a tag on a particular tree, where Taita had buried a million dollars worth of bank notes. The mujeres ironed hundred-dollar bills and slept with the lab technicians, who took coca paste and turned it into crystals of pure cocaine, like the Ticuna doctors had done for a thousand years. It was medicine, not candy to be sold, and they were scornful of Taita's laboratories. But they still considered Taita as an adopted boy cub of their tribe. Taita had rescued these doctors from the little tourist traps outside the town of Benjamín Constant, in Brazil, where they had dressed up for the gringos and did magic tricks, bartered their blowguns and necklaces and ritual masks, until their whole tribal lore was up for sale. Taita had returned them to the rain forest. And they were doctors again, guardians of the Ticuna past.

Then the gold miners had come, with their pans and water pumps, and bottles of liquid mercury to separate the gold from the river sediment, and they hired the witch doctors as gold refiners, and ate into the forests with their mining camps and poisoned the rivers with mercury vapors. The witch doctors were losing their hair and dying of mercury fever until Ruben raided the camps and pushed the miners out. But it was a hopeless war. Taita couldn't police the Amazon. The miners returned with their own independent armies. They had iguanas on their payroll. They bribed the ministers in Bogotá and all six comisarías of the Colombian Amazon. They accused Taita of stealing their gold and destroying their property. And the paisa Robin Hood had another price on his head.

The miners themselves joined the government task forces and the antidrug police to finish Taita and his mythical Dolores once and for all. They massacred acres and acres of forest in pursuit of Taita, trying to encircle him. But he picked up his finca and moved to another part of the forest. And the iguanas mutilated more trees. An entire settlement, two hundred kilometers below a particular camp, succumbed to mercury fever. More and more miners appeared in the Amazon.

And Ruben hobbled around Dolores with the help of his cane. He had his ice cream factory, his birdmen, his cribs of pure cocaine, his cadre of runners and mules, and a fiancée out of his own crazy past. He'd had a hundred sweethearts, mulatas or criollas from Bogotá, mujeres he might have married, but they left no echo in Taita's life. He would dance with them and feel a sadness that nearly tore off his head. He would have to die soon. He had become a little too notorious, even for a traficante. He couldn't run for presidente, like the novelista Bailen Gitano, because he would have been captured while he campaigned. There had been talk of a governmental pardon. But Bailen's own ministers would have toppled him the day he pardoned the paisa Robin Hood. And so Taita withdrew inside himself. He thought about his boyhood in the barrio, the Spanish plains of Nueva York. He only seemed happy now with this strange mujer, Mademoiselle Ramirez, the Christian soldier. She left an echo. But he didn't know how to court his cousin, even though they had been engaged for twenty years. Should he tie her to his bed and make her his concubine. Should he offer her a Swiss account? Should he recite the lines of Bailen Gitano from his great, great novel, *The Fall of the Magicians?* Bailen would win the Primo Nobel one day. "Silvie," says the paisa Robin Hood of Bailen's novel, a traficante like Don Ruben. "Silvie," he says to his sweetheart, a little bogotana, "how can I love you? Even while I breathe I die."

No. He wouldn't quote Bailen. Bailen had betrayed the Greens. Bailen had let the old ministers back into power. And besides, Yolanda might not like such literary stuff. Too bad he didn't have a rumbeadero at Dolores. Then he might have wooed her the Medellín way. But he couldn't keep a staple of musicians at the finca. They weren't guerrilla fighters. They were artists who'd never tolerate the jungle rot or the birdmen, whom they considered cannibals. And the noise of an orchestra would have brought the commandos de la muerte down on his neck. You couldn't have a proper tango in the rain forest. A cine, sí. Because the Ticunas, who loved John Garfield and James Dean, could soundproof one little room in the heart of the finca. And the sound never even touched a single tree.

Stupido, Taita said to himself. Even if he'd had his musicians, he couldn't have done the tango on a pair of burnt and bandaged legs. And he had to approach Yolanda in the midst of all his gloom.

"Little sister," he said, "will you ever think of playing doctor with me again?"

"Cousin, I'm out of practice. I gave up doctor when I got rid of all my dolls . . . anyway, I'd be embarrassed in front of all these men."

"I could build a room for us in the finca."

"Some kind of love nest?"

"Sí."

"Well, I'm not feeling amorous these days. I was sent here by the Christian Commandos to start a dialogue between them and you."

"They're bunglers," Taita said. "*And* Muzo's friend. So how reliable can they be?"

"You were also Muzo's friend. All of you were Greens. You, the comandante, and Professor Sparks."

"El profesor is an imbecile. He's gone into the jungle to make war on the gold miners. He has a permit from Presidente Bailen. And Bailen lets him borrow his environmental cops."

"The miners are just an excuse. I'll bet he's looking for you."

"Sí. With Muzo's men right behind him . . . little sister, would you go with me to Paris?"

"It's just another barrio, Ruben."

"No, no. The best cafeterías have tables with marble tops. And you can have a café con leche and watch all the turistas. In Paris. Or Barcelona. Or Melbourne, Australia, where my family owns two banks."

"Family?" she said. "You mean, your coca cartel."

"No. It's a little family. We could be very rich in Melbourne."

"You're rich right now. You can't even spend all your coca

dollars. And I wouldn't go anywhere with you until you talked to the professor."

She must have seen the sadness in his face, that mark of death he was wearing, long before his "accident" at the Rumbeadero de la Paz, because she kissed him in front of all his men and their mujeres, and it wasn't the kiss of other women, because Yolanda's echo went back twenty years, and he was about to propose marriage when a bullet head cropped up between Yolanda and him. It was the little king, wearing a fiber skirt, his skull painted midnight blue.

"Coño," Ruben muttered, "did you dress up for the turistas?"

"Pappy, there are no turistas here . . . I'm bored."

"But didn't you cry and cry and leave your own army because you wanted to live at the Finca Dolores?"

"I didn't know I'd get the shits from eating ice cream sodas in the jungle."

"There's nothing wrong with my ice cream," Ruben said.

"I'm bored."

"Then I'll have my birdmen take you to Leticia and put you on the plane to Medellín."

"I can't go on a regular flight. I'm a criminal. The iguanas will recognize me at the airport."

"You're an infant," Ruben said. "They'll spank you and send you to an orphanage."

"No, pappy. They'll give me to the commandos de la muerte. The commandos will chop off my head. They'll mount it on a long pole as a lesson to the chinos de la calle."

And it upset Ruben to realize that the little king was right. Ah, he wouldn't be able to propose marriage this afternoon.

Yolanda had that Commando look in her eyes. She was thinking of Sparks, who would rile the gold miners and get everybody killed, including the environmental cops. And here Ruben was, temporarily a cripple. He had the best chemists money could buy. They were all millionaires. They would labor twenty months at the finca and retire to Mazatlan. Should he turn the little king into a chemist? Put him in charge of the movie projector? He'd have to find something for Rudolfo to do.

17

THE REPÚBLICA de Colombia had its own band of Christian soldiers. These environmental rangers were under the Ministry of Agriculture. They wore blue jeans and black headbands. They all carried Colt Commanders. They were a novelista's dream. Presidente Bailen had brought them into the government. They were Bailen's babies. But the rangers teeth were too little. They were one more police force in a land of police. They belonged to Agriculture, but were trained by the minister of justice, who didn't want them to catch any glory. None of them had ever killed a man. They were supposed to fire in the air when they presented their search warrants and busted up the mining camps that were dumping "cooked" mercury into the Amazon waters. But the miners' own mercenaries weren't so polite, and there was a terrific mortality rate among the rangers.

They had few volunteers. The entire cadre was demoralized. Their leader was Leonel Escobar, who was a novelista, like Bailen, and a member of the Greens. He'd arrived with

Professor Sparks at the left bank of the Rio Amacayacu. Escobar had nineteen agents. They were prepared to walk into a camp of a hundred miners, mujeres, and mercenaries. The mujeres were all armed and carried hip holsters like Buffalo Bill. They cooked and panned for gold and slept with the mercenaries and shot environmental agents. The miners handled the mercury.

Leonel watched them with his telescope, while he shared a jungle meal of empanadas and brown sugar sticks with his agents and Professor Sparks. This Sparks was a pain in the ass who liked to talk literature. He'd read all of Leonel's novels and he was an expert on *La caeda del magos*. Bailen's book. It irked Leonel, because he could never live up to *La caeda*. He couldn't tear a book out of his loins the way Bailen did. And now he'd have to endure the professor's litany on Bailen. But Sparks was also a good strategist. Sparks had fought miners up and down the Amazon. And he didn't attempt to bribe the rangers with Yanqui dollars. He seemed to enjoy these missions into the rain forest. He liked to chew on cold empanadas and get shot at by the miners and their mujeres.

"Leonel, we'll have to outflank them, take the bastards by surprise."

"That is difficult when they already know we are here. The mujeres can smell the grease in an empanada a mile away."

"Then we'll have to show them that we mean business."

"How? My minister has not authorized us to kill miners."

"We can maim a couple of mules and blow up the water supply."

"That will only anger them, and the mujeres will take terrible vengeance on my men."

"We'll have to risk it," the professor said. "Bailen's characters love to take risks."

"But that is a romance. And we, señor, are real people."

"Ah, but we still have the mágica of Bailen's book."

The son of a bitch was carrying a stick of dynamite in his pants. If he wasn't careful he'd blow the entire troop of rangers off the bank of the Rio Amacayacu. Never again, Leonel muttered. I will never go on an expedition with this gringo again.

"I forbid the dynamite, Señor Mel. I will not deface the jungle."

"Silly boy," Sparks said. "It's a prop. I swiped it from an acting company in Bogotá. I say we tickle the mothers, bark at them with the nitro in my fist."

Leonel finished his empanada and sucked on a sugar stick. Then he took an electric horn out of his knapsack, signaled to his men, stood high on the bank, and screamed at the miners on the other side of the river.

"Miners of Camp Pacifico, you are under surveillance by environmental officers of the Ministry of Agriculture. I charge you not to resist. We are coming into your camp to inspect the degree of mercury contamination. I repeat. Do not resist."

But Leonel's rangers didn't even get a chance to ford the Rio Amacayacu. The mujeres popped them out of the water like geese. Sparks waved his dynamite stick and the mujeres shot it out of his hand. Instead of their surrounding the miners, the miners surrounded them. Mercenaries stood with assault rifles on the rangers' own river bank.

"Pray, amigos," their chief said. "We do not like the environmentitos." He was a small, ferocious man with one ear, a warrior, while the rangers were not. He was weighted down with ammunition, his own little god. "We do not like them. So get down on your knees and start to pray."

"I'm a United States citizen," Sparks said. "And this is an act of piracy. My government won't stand for it."

"I forgot to bring my chronometer, señor. But you have about five seconds left of breathing time. Start to pray."

Leonel signaled to his men. They got down on their knees like penitents and scratched little crosses into their chests with a fingernail. Sparks wouldn't budge.

"I'm not cowtowing to pirates. I'll take the spears in the chest."

Leonel whispered to him. "They're not carrying spears, Señor Mel. They have assault guns. They will turn your belly into paste . . . and then you will only be a mirage, like Bailen's characters and all his mágica."

"I don't care."

But it was the chief who fell with all his mercenaries, and not Professor Sparks. It was like a jungle fairy tale. Suddenly the chief was standing, and then he was not. He dropped face down into the river bank. Sparks didn't hear a sigh or a groan. It was the best kind of surgical kill. Then he saw a gaggle of blue-faced men behind the fallen mercenaries. With them was Yolanda and a midget, also wearing blue. Sparks recognized the war paint of the Ticunas. They were carrying blowguns. That's what the mágica was about. Poison darts. But what the hell was Yolanda doing here with that midget?

Sparks was amazed at his own acumen. Of course it was Yolanda who led him to the Finca Dolores. Isn't that why he'd brought her to cocaine country in the first place? To arrange a meet with Don Ruben at Dolores, if you could call this cowshed a finca. Sparks wasn't blind to the amenities. He witnessed Ruben's laboratories, and he imagined the tonnage that escaped from such a shed every single week.

The ice cream made him delirious. Passionfruit, he guessed. That was the royal flavor of the month. Ruben didn't arrive until after the ice cream. Must have been arranging his notes in some back room of the hacienda. He was wearing purple pants, like he usually did. And he walked with a limp. Sparks had heard about his wounds. He'd been fried a little at that tango palace on Calle 23. Ruben went up to Leonel, the lord of the environmental rangers, and kissed him on the cheek. They'd been blood brothers once upon a time, fellow Greens until Bailen came into office and realized the rude economics of running a country. Conservative bankers got most of the important ministries. Bailen had cut into the national debt, but not even the gamos of *La caeda* could lower inflation. The dollar had driven the Colombian peso into the back rooms of banking houses.

"Leonel," Ruben said, "say hello to Bailen for me. I have read his last book of stories. I think he should get out of government work, soon as he can."

"We all have to make sacrifices," Leonel said.

The professor was uneasy. He coughed into his hands. "Don Ruben, please. I'm grateful for that rescue party. But we have to talk."

"Sí, señor. Talk."

"In private," Sparks said.

"I have no secrets from my friends."

"Don Ruben, I have a message from the president of the United States. It's a delicate matter."

"You're in my house, el professor. Don't abuse that privilege. I have no secrets."

Sparks wagged his shoulders at Yolanda, but Yolanda wouldn't intervene.

"All right, this is the package. We're prepared for a full pardon. But you have to return with us, settle in the United States . . . Bailen can't afford to have you here. You're stirring up the waters."

"How can I be sure you won't arrest me the minute I arrive in El Norte?"

"Don't you trust the president of the United States?"

"Not if I can help it."

"You were born in Manhattan, for Christ's sake. You lived with us. I mean, Yolanda was the first sweetheart you ever had."

"I'm a citizen of Medellín now."

"You're a little confused. Medellín doesn't issue passports. It's a provincial capital, that's all."

"Not to a paisa."

"But we're in the middle of the Amazon."

"It's business, only business. Business brings me here."

"All right," the professor said. "Tell me what you want."

"A letter of pardon from your president, with the seal of

the United States. I want that letter delivered to Bailen, and countersigned by him. Then it is to be deposited with my lawyer in Basel, Switzerland. I'll give you the address."

"Your lawyer's in Basel?"

"Professor Sparks, I have lawyers everywhere."

"All right. What else?"

"I will only go to North America en famille."

"I don't understand."

"With King Rudolfo and Yolanda Ramirez."

"I can't control Yolanda. She's a citizen of the United States."

"A little frankness, professor. She works for you and she has a prison sentence hanging over her head. I want a full pardon."

"All right. But who's this King Rudolfo?"

Taita pointed to the midget with the blue face. And then Leonel whispered in Sparks' ear. The professor closed his eyes.

"Jesus, that's a murderer."

"He's seven years old."

The professor opened his eyes again. "I can't steal him from Colombia."

"He comes with us."

"Understood. But no more cocaine, or we will bust your ass. You're out of business. Retired. And the president will expect you to make personal appearances so he can clarify the nature of your pardon. He's taking a gamble, Ruben."

"No, señor. I'm going to save his fucking skin."

ROBIN HOOD

18

H E H A D dinner at the White House, without Yolanda
or the little king. It was in the Rose Room, and Taita recog-
nized Franklin D. Roosevelt on the wall. El inválido mag-
nifico. Taita had to shed his purple pants for the occasion.
He arrived with Bruno West, boss of the Christian Comman-
dos. Sparks hadn't been invited. But Sparks had coached
him and found him a tailor. Ruben wore a white dinner
jacket. He didn't need a Baptist preacher's boy like Sparks
to teach him table manners. He'd been all over the world as
a traficante. He'd saved his silk napkin from the lunch he'd
had with some princess of the Rothschilds on the Île-St.-
Louis. And he'd sat at the table where Napoleon used to sit
with his empress, Josephine, at le Grand Véfour, a restaurant
with little red curtains.

He shook hands with the president and kissed the First
Lady on the cheek, congratulated her on her silverware, as
Sparks had told him to do. He gave her a first edition of *La
caeda del magos,* because she was a fan of Bailen's and a

voracious reader. He talked to a man from the Army War College who admired the guerrilla priests.

"Some of them are Dominicans, yes?"

"I think so, señor."

"Do they fight in their habits?"

"No, señor. They have given up their vows. Colombia is a civilized country, señor. A priest is not permitted to kill."

"But what if they defied the Church?"

"They love the Church, señor. And they could not recite the Mass with the memory of blood on their hands."

"Not even Christ's blood?"

"You are provoking me, señor. I am a believer."

The butlers wore blue. Taita drank white wine with his fish. He didn't burp once.

"Why do they call you Taita?" the First Lady asked him during dessert.

"*Taita* comes from the barrios, Madame President. It means little father. The campesinos use it a lot. In my case, it is a matter of affection. I get along with children."

"But it isn't only children who call you Taita."

"Yes, that's true."

"He cares about the poor, isn't that right?" said Bruno West.

"Many people care about the poor," Taita said.

"He's the Robin Hood of all the paisas, aren't you, Ruben?"

"Stop prompting him, Bruno," said the president. "He isn't a boy. I don't want him rehearsed."

"Thank you, Mr. President," said Robin Hood, who was beginning to enjoy himself among all these North American knights. But the Yankees didn't know how to cook. He'd had a better meal in the darkest cantina. The fish had no sausages on the side. The flan was without flavor. And the ice cream was as exotic as a fig. But the company was good. Mrs. Fannie Morrison, big mama of the Environmental Protection Agency, was a bit of a leech. She couldn't stop making eyes at Ruben. She pressed him while he drank his coffee, which was little more than poisoned milk and would have caused a scandal in Medellín.

"Are you really a Green?"

"Mrs. Fannie," he said, "I have killed to protect the environment. I have strangled with my hands the tombos who have poisoned our rivers and our wells."

Bruno was quietly having a heart attack.

"What's a tombo?" Mrs. Fannie asked.

"A policeman who is also part of a death squad."

"I know President Bailen," she said, her eyes flashing all sorts of crazy sexual colors. "He's a humanitarian. He wouldn't condone death squads in his government."

"Mrs. Fannie, the death squads were there before Bailen, and they'll be with us after he's gone. It's frontier justice, Medellín style."

The president was pleased with his new "purchase." He smoked a cigar and invited Ruben into his study. He was the first Democrat to reach the White House since the long days and nights of Jimmy Carter. The country was undecided about him. He'd had a short honeymoon with the American public, and then his popularity began to fall.

The White House had become a Roosevelt museum. He had images of FDR all over the place. The president would have liked to start his own New Deal. But he couldn't find the motor. Europe was a bigger economic force than the

United States. Japan had franchised half the world. The deutsche mark was crippling the dollar, and was now the preferred currency. The Arabs were drifting into their own messianic void. Africa was starving to death. And the Latin Americans were waiting for some kind of leadership from El Jefe of the North. Congress was biting his back. The Russkies were entering a dark age of internal strife. The president was feeding them corn and Coca Cola. He was sixty-six years old. He was decent, courageous, this ex-governor of Idaho. He could have chased Robin Hood to the ends of the earth. Bogotá had agreed to extradite the boy, but it couldn't seem to find him. Neither could the DEA. The Drug Enforcement people had sent their scalp-hunters into the jungle, had promised to deliver Ruben's head on a plate, and hadn't even come up with a piece of his shirt.

So the president had to take the initiative. He'd pardoned Taita. And he was hoping his popularity would rise on the strength of this Green traficante.

"Reporters will hound you, Ruben. They'll be merciless about the cocaine. I've guaranteed them that all your dealing is in the past . . . don't make a liar out of me."

The man with the cigar had touched Ruben. He hadn't expected to like El Jefe. But there was a kind of elemental kinship between them. The presidency had become a brutal trap. Pax Americana couldn't rule a kindergarten class. And the president had to tapdance all the time, without one foot knowing where the other foot would land.

He'd never intended to give up cocaine. The cartel operated at a distance from Ruben. His profits were a million a day.

He'd still have to die. All it took was one greedy traficante. But perhaps he could dodge the Devil for a little while. El Presidente had become a tremendous cloak. Now Ruben had to live the life of a Green.

But the Devil had found the means to twist his heart. Because Taita was fond of this second Franklin Roosevelt. He hadn't expected that. He would have been happier if the president had mocked him. But they were like two little men in a boat, and it was sink or swim, sink or swim.

Taita cut his profits in half. He broke all the ties he had, except with his lawyer in Basel, who managed his legitimate accounts. The banks he'd bought in Melbourne were worth a billion, and they'd stopped laundering money for the cartel. And so he was sitting pretty until some governmental task force broke through all of Ruben's screens and traced him back to the cartel.

Meanwhile he rocked in the world's cradle. The media couldn't get enough of him. He was on the covers of *Time* and *Der Spiegel.* Two hundred feature articles appeared the week of his pardon. But the furor didn't die down. It seemed to intensify with every trip to a television studio. He was Robin Hood, after all. His purple pants lent him a primitive charm.

Some journalist called him a Latino Gatsby, and the name held. He was offered movie contracts. Ruben had no desire to act. ABC begged him to dance the tango in their studios, but he declined. He could only do the tango medellín in Medellín. And now he lived in the United States. His refusal to dance only fired up the imagination of America. The public dreamt of him as a tango king, and that was much more powerful than anything ABC could have done.

Tango dancers everywhere began to put on purple pants. Ruben wouldn't sell his own likeness. He did no commercials. He wouldn't answer questions outside his own expertise. He was a Green. He talked about the planet. He talked about Colombian cocaine. He lied as little as he could about the cartel.

He didn't beat his chest, like some reformers. "I was poor," he said. "I lived on the street. And cocaine was the business of the street. You had two or three choices in Medellín. You could become a tombo or a priest or go into cocaine. I make no apologies. I killed in order not to be killed."

And there was always that other nagging question. How did a druglord become a Green? His nostrils would widen. He would touch the pleat in his purple pants. "I am a paisa, and paisas have always been Greens. My grandfathers never ruined the countryside. We didn't keep slaves. We didn't exploit the Indios. None of us grew rich on the backs of other men. Yes, I was a traficante. But I did not breathe mercury into our rivers. I destroyed no forests. The ground is holy to all paisas . . ."

19

THE PRESIDENT'S popularity began to grow. He was the man who had rescued the paisa Robin Hood from a life of crime. He'd pardoned Ruben, given him to the people of the United States, this tango king who wouldn't dance. Bruno West was a little piqued. "We do all the work, we train Yolanda, we find Ruben in the rain forest, and—"

"Sir," Sparks said, "Ruben found us."

"Never mind. We dig around in the dirt, and he comes up smelling like a rose. He reaps all the rewards."

"He is the president of the United States. And he did sponsor our mission."

"With pennies," Bruno said. "He's a stingy one, that old man."

The president was three years younger than Bruno West, but Sparks didn't argue the point. "We've also benefited, sir. They're much nicer to us on the Hill."

"Stop calling me sir, for God's sake. Tell me, Sparks, what do you make of the little shit? Our Robin Hood, I mean. I don't really like him."

"He hasn't strayed, Bruno. I would have caught him."

"Oh, he'll follow the letter of the law. We've given him a gold mine. He doesn't have to fiddle with cocaine. But my friends at the Bureau have been grumbling. You can't just break away from the cartel. It's like our own Maf. Blood ties and everything. And the Medellín boys are much more vicious. They kill entire families . . . and here's our lad, winking at the cameras like God's own little angel. What do you think?"

The professor had been suspicious all along, but he didn't want to send Bruno out barking into the corridors of D.C. The Christian Commandos had a decent budget for the first time. Money was pouring in. They could outfit a small army at their tidewater retreat. There were other Rubens, other Robin Hoods.

"Well, what do you think?"

"I'm not worried about Don Ruben. We can always chop off his legs."

"That's the ticket, Sparks. Only I wouldn't bet on it. That boy's been running a coca corporation almost as big as General Motors. Do you have him under surveillance?"

"All the time."

Bruno picked up his pipe and went to have lunch with the secretary of state. And Sparks caught the 1 p.m. shuttle to New York. He read an article about Ruben on the plane. He'd have to add it to his files. The Commandos already had an enormous dossier on Don Ruben, a bloody book, like a lunatic chapter out of *La caeda del magos,* but without Bailen's genius. This article was in *Esquire.* It had the obligatory photograph of Ruben in his purple pants. "The Great Gatsby of the Spanish-American Steppes."

Damn inaccurate if you ask me. Medellín wasn't part of any tundra. And Ruben wasn't Jay Gatsby or Michael Strogoff or Benya Krik. He was a homeboy who happened to make good. But if the press romanticized Ruben, wasn't the professor himself to blame? He'd nurtured the image, got Bruno to harp about Ruben in the president's ear. Now the homeboy was one more media monster, like Madonna or Andy Warhol's ghost.

Sparks had a limousine waiting for him at La Guardia. One more bonus of the new Commandos. He didn't have to beg or borrow from Justice and State. The White House gave him whatever he wanted.

He rode into town. He had his man park in a little garage across from Tompkins Square. Ruben had a penthouse apartment for Yolanda and the little king in the Latino Lower East Side. It had become a neighborhood of Caribbean grocers on the rise and gringo artists or account execs who liked the idea of living in a converted slum. There was always salsa in the streets. The grocers had palm trees painted in their windows. And Sparks could buy chorizos or snow cones from any vendor. Loisaida had been cocaine country once upon a time, and perhaps it still was. The professor hadn't talked to his informants at the DEA in a while. But it didn't have the despair of the uptown barrios. Because it was a little too close to the fatlands of Manhattan, and it was becoming a fatland of its own.

He rang Yolanda's bell and climbed up to the penthouse. He'd have to do a month of basic at the farm, because he was winded when he got to the top of the stairs. And he was guilty as hell. Her child was still entangled in the courts, and Yolanda had never received an official parole. If Ruben misbehaved, the little daughter would go back to Harrington Hills.

"How are you, Yolandie? You're looking great."

He desired her, but he couldn't afford to mix politics and pleasure. He was sleeping with a government girl from K Street twice a month, and that was all the intimacy he could bear.

The little daughter had dark spots under her eyes.

"Professor, when am I going to get my Benjamin back?"

"We're working on it."

He wasn't, of course. He needed the leverage of a lost boy. Even an environmentalist had to have a strategic program. Lives were commodities most of the time. And he was a Commando. He had to take risks.

"If you don't bring me my boy, I'm going to steal him from Family Court. It's only fair. The court stole him from me."

"Ah, but the judge won't look at it like that . . . where's the little king?"

"I'm not sure. He disappears and comes home for supper once a week. He has to be a chino de la calle no matter where he is."

"But if he gets in trouble, Yolanda, if he robs or kills another chino, we'll all be up the creek. He has a rather peculiar status in the U.S.A. Sort of the president's guest, but he doesn't really exist."

"I'm not his watchdog, professor. I only fix his meals."

"What about Prince Charming?"

"Ruben? He's on the road a lot. I have a café con leche with him between his television gigs."

"Don't mean to pry, Yolanda. But I have to ask you a personal question. Has Ruben been sleeping with you?"

She socked him in the face with a closed fist. The professor landed on his ass. His jaw began to quiver. Ah, she punched like a Commando. Good girl, Yolanda, good girl.

She leaned over him with some kind of sorrow.

"You shouldn't ask a chica questions like that."

She made him an ice pack, helped him to his feet, sat him in her favorite chair, and applied the ice to his jaw, which was still quivering. The view from Yolanda's window was fabulous. He could see across the park, into a landscape of low red roofs, like jagged teeth.

"Yolanda, I'm sorry. But I have to know. Did you spend one night with him?"

"Sí."

"In the same bed?"

She puckered her lip as she pondered. "Sí. He was gentle, professor. He kissed my eyes. He didn't look under my night dress. We smoked a little grass . . . 'marimba' he called it. Then he put out the lights."

"And he didn't make love."

"No . . . not if you want to be technical. Now get out of my face, Professor Sparks. And don't you dare come back without my Benjamin."

20

H E H A D Ruben's days and nights marked down in his own agenda. The tango king was in tinseltown. It seemed right. Ruben had marketed himself the way a Hollywood mogul might have marketed a man. What was it that Thalberg or Zanuck had once said? "It takes ten years to make a star overnight." Ruben was his own Zanuck, with a little help from the Christian Commandos and the president of the United States. He'd come to address the Sierra Club, the Los Angeles Conservation Society, the Motion Picture and Television Artists for a Green Planet, the East L.A. Chapter of Chicanoland, the Z Channel, and the Friends of the *Los Angeles Times*.

Sparks had arranged most of the bookings. He'd been sentimental enough to think of himself as Ruben's mentor, a kind of benevolent coach who could steer Don Ruben through the briar patches of gringo society. But the homeboy didn't need Sparks. He had all of Hollywood eating out of his hand.

Chicano gangs serenaded him from their armed jeeps.

Synagogues along Rodeo Drive welcomed him as a South American son. He was seen at the Hollywood Bowl with environmental rat packs. He watched Marlon Brando play Simón Bolívar on the back lots of Warner Bros., in an adaptation of Bailen's first novel, *A Cavalry of Swans*.

Brando weighed three hundred pounds. He was seventy, but he looked like that gallant horseman. He rode a pinto on the set. He wore white gloves and a jacket high at the neck. His jowls meant nothing. He was Bolívar.

Ruben started to cry.

"What's wrong?" Brando asked, he who lived like an exile in the Santa Monica Mountains.

"I was scared," Ruben said. "I thought I was in the middle of a dream."

"That's the movies. I'm only a mumbler. I prance around like an ape."

"No, hermano. An ordinary mumbler wouldn't behave like El Libertador."

He was haunted the whole afternoon, even when he spoke at the Beverly Wilshire to the Daughters of the Golden West. "I'm not a hero," he insisted. "I'm just a man who's been pardoned by the president of the United States."

He recognized a preacher at the back of the room.

Sparks had arrived in Hollywood that afternoon. "Son of a bitch," he muttered to himself. "Our homeboy has the modesty of a tarantula."

Ruben walked into the bar after the Daughters went home and found Sparks drinking vodka martinis and stuffing pretzels into his mouth.

"Professor, you shouldn't be doing that."

"I know. I'm an alcoholic. I'll have to run to an A.A.

153

meeting after I get out of here . . . I met some wonderful chaps at the A.A. in Medellín. They thought the world of you. 'Rubenito,' they said. 'He is Guillermo Gaudí and Simón Bolívar and Robin Hood and Mickey Rourke.' But I didn't tell them that you were also the rat bastard Judas of Medellín."

"El Profesor, I'll take you back to your hotel."

"Don't have one. This is only a day trip . . . not that I couldn't afford the Bev Hilton or the Wilshire. You're making us rich." He clutched Ruben's hand. "Top of the world, isn't it, Robin Hood? I was your perfect patsy."

"No," Ruben said, retrieving his own hand. "You're just a Baptist who latched onto a holy cause. And I was part of the picture."

"You used us, Ruben."

"Professor, it was a two-way street."

"All that talk about a childhood sweetheart. You planted little poison kisses. You had us find Yolanda. She means nothing to you."

"You're wrong, Professor."

"Yes, hearts and flowers, little brother. We saved your ass. We got you out of cocaine country. It was a used-up career. And now you're the darling of America, the president's fair-haired boy."

"I have a dark complexion, señor."

"You know what the fuck I mean. Bailen was squeezing you, wasn't he? He couldn't clean up the coca with you around."

"Imbecile," Ruben said. "Bailen was part of my band. He worked for me before he got the presidential bug."

"I don't believe it. He's the foremost novelist in South America."

"He was my coca man in Cartagena. It was coca that allowed him to write, coca that supported his family, until the gringos discovered *La caeda* and called him a great man. I could have blown his head off, but I let him have his little game of independence. I contributed to his campaign. And then he decided he would enter the community of nations as the man who brought down the cartel. It's all a mirage, Professor. Medellín is numero uno, even with all the civil wars."

"But you decided to get out."

"Sí, I was sick of jungle ice cream. I wanted more than a finca in the wilderness."

"And so you cultivated yourself as a Green."

"I could pluck your eyes out with two fingers, señor."

"I'm a Commando," Sparks said. "Don't forget."

"And a Boy Scout who fights gold miners with fake sticks of dynamite . . . Professor, there would have been no Green Party in Colombia without the cartel. How were the Greens financed? By Ruben Falcone. I had no hidden motives. I didn't want honor or respectability."

"Just a mechanism for getting out. You discovered the Christian Commandos. And you climbed onto our backs, with Yolanda as the bait. She loves you . . . didn't you hear me? Yolanda loves you."

The tango king smiled. "I heard you, El Profesor. I got her out of your Yankee jail, didn't I? She saw the Amazon. She visited our little cocaine capital. She had her banana splits. She even danced the tango medellín."

"And nearly got blown up."

"I was in the same explosion, señor. It was the work of your friend, Muzo the Magnificent."

"He's not my friend."

"You brought Yolanda to Medellín on his plane."

"The man is acting minister of justice."

"And chief architect of Medellín's new commandos de la muerte."

"You had your own death squads."

"I killed tombos, not innocent people."

"It's always the other side that kills los inocentes. But tell me, heart to heart, do you love Yolanda?"

"Yes and no."

"That's not good enough. You're on my shit list, starting today. You never ended things with the cartel. You're still a coca man. And I'm gonna prove it."

"Really, Professor? And break the president's heart."

"You son of a bitch."

"You're my lecture agent, my guide in America. Don't forget."

The professor returned to Q Street. There was a funny guy waiting at his door. A European, Sparks figured, because the guy's umbrella was furled so tight, it looked like an enormous leather pin.

"I'm Karl Erasmus Levi."

"Ah, Robin Hood's lawyer, I presume. The man from Basel."

"May I come in?"

"I'm tired, Mr. Erasmus Levi. I got off the plane from

Los Angeles. Couldn't we diddle around some other time."

"I'm due back in Basel. You're familiar with the Washington law firm of Weissbroner and Hale. They're acting as our agents. The firm is helping us prepare our briefs. It will be quite an interesting case. *Yolanda Ramirez* v. *the United States of America.* May I come in?"

Sparks invited the man from Basel upstairs to his attic office. They sat facing each other, a little desk between them. The desk also served as Sparks' dining table."

"I'm eager to know, Mr. Sparks, if presidents of the United States are in the habit of kidnapping female convicts?"

"No one kidnapped Yolanda."

"Indeed. I had Weissbroner do a thorough check. And there is no record of her parole."

"Mr. Erasmus Levi, I'm not sure how they do things in Basel. But you're treading pretty close to the Official Secrets Act."

"Ah, and you will claim that Ms. Ramirez is vital to the national security. Good. And Mr. Falcone too? Since his life today is little more than a popularity contest for the president."

"I don't get it. I thought Ruben was your client."

"Not in this case."

"You're bluffing," Sparks said. "Weissbroner and Hale aren't kamikaze pilots. They wouldn't be dumb enough to try and sue the president."

"But we aren't suing the president. We'll expose the Christian Commandos, and their front, the Phalanx Project."

"We aren't a governmental agency. So you're back to zero, Mr. Erasmus Levi."

"I think not. There's a rather bizarre chain between the White House and the Christian Commandos . . . we'll pull on that chain and see what happens."

"What do you want?"

"Parole for Ms. Ramirez, effective immediately. And full custody of her child."

"The boy's a bastard. I'm going to have a hard time convincing the courts to give him back."

"I'm sure you'll manage. You have quite a lot of resources on your side."

The man from Basel picked up his umbrella and let himself out of Commando headquarters.

Sparks' temples began to pound. He was going to have the headache of his life.

THE BLUES BROTHERS

21

H E WAS tittering at some edge of excitement, him
with the purple pants. How could he ever complain? The
world had become a huge tit for him to pull on. And Robin
Hood pulled and pulled. He wasn't a paisa anymore. He was
the king of all countries, the dancer who didn't have to
dance. But he was having bad dreams, nightmares that
would send him howling into the streets at 4 a.m. to look for
a comforting soul. He couldn't find much comfort on the
Strip, just wayfarers like himself, perhaps even an ex-paisa.

He lived at the Château Marmont, in the same bungalow
where John Belushi had died. Ruben wasn't bothered by
Belushi's ghost. He wouldn't dream about strangers, even
though he'd seen *The Blues Brothers* seven times at the cines
of Medellín when he was a little boy who'd arrived from El
Norte with his dad. "Pappy's a paisa, pappy's a paisa," he'd
announce to himself, as if he'd discovered the wonders of
the word. His dad couldn't tolerate the climate of the North.
Falcone Sr. had a constant whooping cough. He was a car-
penter who'd gone north to live in a colony of paisas and

earn his bread. But El Norte didn't have the Sinfonía de Luces. It didn't have the tango medellín. It had snow and cucarachas and backbreaking work where a man could not get a union card and had to slave for some Latino boss. Falcone Sr. earned his bread, but he coughed and coughed.

Ruben remembered the dry, hacking cough, that was like death's own little finger. He'd cried when he left the barrio and his sweetheart Yolanda, whom he intended to marry once he grew up a little and became a carpenter like his dad. He cried in Medellín, but he got used to the paisas. And for him *The Blues Brothers* was like the America he had lost, loud and a little crazy.

In his dream Taita started to dance. He was Guillermo Gaudí's heir. Foolishly he took the tango wherever he went. He danced at rumbeaderos all over the world. But the tango medellín was only a ruse. He dealt drugs at the rumbeaderos. He had his accountant and his birdmen, who were his bodyguards. His bodyguards starved to death because they could not find nourishment in the food of Delhi or Rome or Perth. The ice cream lacked the proper roots. And Taita hadn't understood their diseases in time, a sickness of the psyche that took the form of unattainable ice cream.

He would look at the death masks the birdmen themselves had prepared in their fall from paradise, the gnarled, twisted faces without any eyes, and he would wake up and run to the mirror, searching for his eyes, and then he'd start to prowl in the foothills of Hollywood. "Pappy is a paisa, Pappy is a paisa," he'd cry, like some lunatic reciting his beads. His pappy had gone home to do the tango and die. But Taita had no home, and the Devil was right behind his back . . .

❧

Bailen wasn't doing so bravely without the tango king. The civil war had worsened in Medellín. The death squads had multiplied. There was no money, American, German, or Swiss. All currency had disappeared from the streets. "Ah," Taita said, watching the nine o'clock news in his bungalow at the Marmont and gobbling a TV dinner, with its wonderful little tin tray for the peas and the mashed potatoes and the roast turkey in cream sauce. "Ah, the putas are hoarding their dollar bills."

It was an eight-minute report on the crisis in Colombia. Taita watched the corpses on the Avenida Junin and couldn't even cry. Some mechanism inside himself had been shut off. He watched Bailen deliver a speech from the steps of the Palacio Presidential in Bogotá, with a bulletproof shield in front of the microphone and soldiers in crash helmets all around him. Bailen's voice began to falter. His eyes seemed orange in Taita's screen. "We cannot give in to the brutos," he said.

"Imbécil," Taita shouted at the screen. "You are the bruto. You should have stayed with your books."

There were images of Bailen's soldiers in the Amazon, looking for cocaine farms and fincas. There were images of gold miners, leering at the camera as they mixed their mercury solutions. There were images of los chinos de la calle in the alleys of Bogotá, with dark faces and dirty hands, huddling next to a bonfire.

The commentator said, "Colombia 1995. Like Humpty Dumpty, ready to fall. Two years ago the world applauded the victory of Bailen's Green Party. It was the first time that the Greens had occupied a presidential palace. But the victory has borne very little fruit. The country still does not have its own minister of the environment. Many people feel that Bailen has betrayed his original mandate. He has reduced the debt, but at what price? Leftist guerrillas control half the countryside. Death squads are rampant everywhere. There are four hundred thousand homeless children in Bogotá alone. Medellín is little more than an armed camp. The Palacio de Justicia in Bogotá, seized by guerrillas in 1992, still sits in its own ruin on the north side of the Plaza de Bolivar. More than anything in the land it is a symbol of the country's endless strife and civil war.

"Just four months ago, after Christmas, there was a bit of hope. Ruben Falcone, chief of the Medellín cartel and the world's richest druglord, abandoned his base in the Amazon, withdrew from the cartel, and arrived in the United States with a presidential pardon. Taita, as he's called, has always been a controversial figure. He started the Green Party, with blessings from the cartel. He constructed entire barrios for Medellín's poor. And it was believed that this voluntary retirement would signal a concordat between the government in Bogotá and the Medellín cartel, a winding down of the drug trade. But it isn't so. Eduardo 'Dancer' Magallon, has seized control of the cartel. And the Dancer has declared his own bloody war. Twice as much cocaine is being processed in the Dancer's cribs. He's—"

Taita switched off the tube. "Mr. Television Man, it's not the Dancer's fault. Muzo's making trouble."

But Taita had to be sure. He sent a fax to Switzerland. He loved this new electronic world. He could cut a man's heart out in the distance between two commas or semicolons. He waited by the pool. He had a Coca Cola, Medellín's favorite drink. The concierge brought him the reply to his fax: it was a flight number. He slept in his bungalow, ate at a kosher delicatessen on Sunset, because he'd developed an appetite for that hebreo empanada called a knish. He avoided the Palais de la Colombie, which was across the street from his hotel. Its food was neither Colombian nor French, but a little dream of the Andes and the Amazon, with plantains and grilled bananas and rice cooked in coconut milk. It was Hollywood's call of the wild. Taita preferred a knish.

He drove out to L.A. International, sat in a lounge, and waited for the Air Panama flight from Mexico City. An hombre in purple pants, identical to Taita's, did a curious tango at the gate, weaving around half a dozen other passengers. He wore dark glasses and a porkpie hat. Ruben donned his own dark glasses and the little hat he'd carried with him from the alleys of Medellín. Now they looked like twins.

"Hello, Dancer," Ruben said. They kissed on the mouth, the Medellín way. Not like maricons, but like hombres who had killed together and would have gladly died to earn such a kiss. They were the Blues Brothers of Colombian cocaine, traficantes who'd presided over an empire. Dancer Magallon was five years older than Don Ruben. He had a tiny scar along his right cheek, but the scar didn't make him menacing. His eyes were blue under the glasses. He'd been Ruben's "warlord," his strategist and chief assassin. And he ruled now, during Taita's exile. The Dancer was scrupulous about money. He would never cheat another traficante, or renege on a bribe that was due. Their only contact now was via Ruben's lawyer.

"Dancer," Ruben said, "I love it here. It's like a barrio with bright lights. Come, I'll show you Hollywood."

"Hombre, you forget. I've done business on these streets."

Of course. The Dancer had iced a police spy in a parking lot on Hollywood Boulevard. In the old days, long before Bailen, he would commute between Panama and Los Angeles, conferring with the cartel's California interests.

They could have done all their talking at the airport, but they were old friends and had to share something together. A woman? The Dancer had a family and would not visit putas. He'd never been unfaithful to his wife. Drugs? He didn't like to do cocaine on a business trip. And so Eduardo Magallon took Don Ruben to a cantina in East L.A., where they ate and drank until their bellies hurt. The Dancer didn't even have to break a twenty-dollar bill. The owner wouldn't accept money from the Blues Brothers.

Taita signed the menu, but the Dancer didn't.

"Hermano," he said to the owner. "It would be a capital offense. I'm not supposed to exist in the United States. I'm a very dangerous man."

The Dancer did one small tango with the owner's wife. He wasn't as strict as Taita about where he danced. Taita was only promiscuous in his dreams. Eduardo gave the owner's wife a ring he'd worn for twenty years. Then he sat down with Taita, and the Blues Brothers were left alone.

"We miss our Taita. We had to learn his tactics all over again."

"I told you to consult my lawyer. I was willing to help."

"We wouldn't interfere with your retreat in North America . . . have any of our payments been short?"

"No," Taita said.

"Have we offended you? Have we been impolite?"

"No."

"Then, hijueputa, why did you bring me here?"

"I saw something on the television . . ."

"I risk my ass," the Dancer said, "come to a country that wants my blood, because you saw something on the television? Hermano, what did you see? A little more of a massacre? Bailen crying to the cameras? What did you expect? Muzo is greedy. He takes our bribes and still tries to kill us."

"Then kill him. You have the money and the means. We've killed ministers and generals before."

"I can't. Muzo runs more and more of our dope. We would collapse without his planes."

"Then I don't understand this war."

"Hermano, did you become a niña in the United States? Muzo wants to be president. We're helping him destabilize the country."

"What about Bailen?"

"Bailen betrayed us. He fed us to the Drug Enforcement people. He signed the extradition papers. You are free. But not everyone is Taita."

"If Bailen falls, the tombos will come back."

"Open your eyes, my friend. The tombos were always there."

"And what will happen to the Green Party?"

"Que putería! The Greens lived off our treasure chest. I don't send helicopters and bulldozers into the forests."

"What deal have you made with Muzo?"

The Dancer looked into Ruben's eyes.

"What deal have you made?"

"We discredit El Presidente and all the Greens. The government collapses. Muzo arrests Bailen. We lock him in a room and let him write his novels. No harm with come to Bailen, I swear."

"Eduardo, I want this stopped."

"You cannot dictate. You abandoned us. I did not ask to sit where I am sitting."

"I want it stopped."

"It has already been decided, Taita. Don't ask me to tell you lies."

The Blues Brothers returned to the airport.

"If you come back to Medellín, Taita, I'll have to kill you."

They kissed. The Dancer boarded the plane. Taita could read the kiss. The Dancer conceded nothing. He meant to kill him, whether Taita returned to Medellín or not. And he wanted Taita to know that *before* he got on the plane.

That's how the Blues Brothers waged a war.

22

H E D I D N ' T have to fiddle around on the phone. He called the president's private line. And the president didn't consult any calendars or switch him to his personal secretary. He invited Robin Hood to spend the night. A limousine met him at Dulles International. The president had already gone to bed. A cup of hot chocolate was waiting for Ruben in one of the anterooms off the kitchen. He was given towels and a toothbrush. It thrilled Ruben. He was just a little boy in the president's house. He slept in the Andrew Jackson bedroom, in a pair of the president's own pajamas.

They had breakfast on the north veranda, without a single aide. The president piped the breakfast orders into the air, and then a young marine arrived with two breakfast trays. This marine was part of the "perimeter." He saluted the president and disappeared.

They both had bacon and eggs.

"Damn if I'll worry about cholesterol," the president said. "I've had bacon since I was born and I'm still alive. The trick is to eat a grapefruit. It drowns all the fat."

"Mr. President, you have to send me back to Colombia."

"Don't interrupt me, son. I'm giving you a sermon on food and American culture. We eat our bacon and survive. We work hard, we don't like other men to see our women's breasts, and we prefer our presidents to be tall. Truman was a short man. Congress gave him hell. Carter was short, and he had to run home to peanutland. I'm a tall Democrat, and I don't intend to rot . . . give me one reason why I should trust you? You are the cartel. Some of my lads from the Secret Service saw you sitting at the airport with Dancer Magallon. You had the L.A. field office jumping for weeks. That's the reward you get. The Secret Service has been looking after you as a favor to their president. We were getting tips that you might be in trouble. And I know about all the nuts that are out there. Damn it, Ruben, for a minute I thought you were my future. I couldn't even let my boys arrest the Dancer. It would have tied him to my Green friend, Ruben Falcone, and embarrassed the heck out of me. So we let the little fucker go through the gate . . . now why should I trust you?"

"You shouldn't. But Bailen's in deep shit."

"Hell, we know that."

"He hasn't taken a penny from the cartel since he was elected. If you're banking on Muzo, don't. He'll start his own cartel, the guerrillas will go crazy, and Colombia will drop off the map."

"Bailen doesn't like you. He wouldn't want you around. And I can't just slip you back in. That would be illegal."

"I want to be Bailen's minister for the environment."

"He hasn't named one yet. And it's unlikely he'll name you."

"Then breathe on him, Mr. President. Because I'm going back."

"I believe you. You know, we taped every word you had with the Dancer. We planted bullet mikes in front of you, behind you, everywhere. The mikes are sensational. And you were almost eloquent. So was the Dancer. And if you ever come back to my country, Ruben, I'll break your fucking neck."

※

By that evening it was done. Bailen agreed to take him into his cabinet as acting minister of environmental affairs, which didn't mean much, because there was no permanent ministry for the environment. But at least Taita would have his own little flag and an office in the president's palace, where he wouldn't be a nuisance to the other ministers.

He couldn't run away without notifying the little king. But where to find Rudolfo? Ruben scoured Loisaida. It was like a return to the navel. He remembered all the mean little streets. His pappy had worked for a Latino carpenter on Pitt Street when Ruben was a baby boy. Falcone Sr. would carry him on his back and explore Loisaida for salvageable sticks of wood. And Ruben hadn't lost that sense of detail when he'd been his father's little helper. And so he looked and looked.

Loisaida had its own chinos de la calle. Ah, but he could not compare this to the Medellín variety. These niños had a home. But they liked to pilfer in the streets. They collected around trash cans and enjoyed their own winter fire. Their faces were relatively clean. Their nails weren't crusted with dirt. They were gringos with a Latino flavor. And none of them was a girl.

He bribed them with gringo dollars.

"I need the little king . . . he calls himself Rudolfo. He's seven, but he looks five or six. He attacks with sharp glass, and he has a sharper set of teeth. He's bitten through an awful lot of throats."

But the chinos hadn't seen Rudolfo. And Ruben wondered if the little king had become a lone wolf in North America, without a gallada of his own.

Ruben's heart was racing and he didn't know why. Hombres were already following him. They could have been Eduardo's men or agents of the Secret Service. How could he tell one from the other? The hombres wore dark coats and rubber boots to grab against the snow on the ground. Ruben had his own sharp teeth. But he didn't want to become the assassin of the North.

The little king had vanished from the streets. And Ruben despaired. Because the Dancer would attack his little family. The Dancer was malicious. His assassins would wait and wait until the little king surfaced for a glass of water or some gringo ice cream.

"Ah, I can't go to Bogotá without him."

An hombre appeared behind Ruben in those galoshes of the North. And then Ruben saw a great whirling object, like a fireball. The fireball fell on top of the hombre. And suddenly Ruben could discern arms and teeth.

"Don't," he shouted. "Rudolfo, please."

And the little king came to rest on top of the hombre, who removed a badge from inside his coat with one shivering paw. "Matlock," he said. "Secret Service."

Ruben sniffed the badge. That was enough. He didn't have to read what was on it.

"Mr. Secret Service man, you're trespassing on a family affair. I have some personal business with this boy."

"Well, sir . . ."

"I know, the president's concerned about my life. But I have Rudolfo. He's all the army I require. Goodbye."

Rudolfo climbed off the Secret Service man, who scrambled to his feet and tramped off into the snow. The boy seemed wilder in El Norte. His hair was uncombed. He didn't have the confidence of his own territory.

"Brujo, why didn't you say hello? You saw I was looking for you."

"Because there were strange men behind you."

"Ah, so you've been following me while I did my own little dance."

"You weren't dancing, pappy."

"Yes, I was. I'm going to Bogotá. I want you to come."

"No, pappy. I'll stay here. I haven't explored enough."

"You must be hard of hearing. That wasn't a request. It's a command."

"You can't command a king."

"Then I'll put it another way. You'll have to tear my throat off, because I'm not leaving without you."

"I would never harm you, pappy."

"I'm glad. Bailen has made me one of his ministers. I want you with me."

"Pappy, I'm on everybody's death list."

"Not now. I negotiated for you. Bailen hates us both. But what can he do?"

"I've never been to Bogotá."

"It's one more Babylon. Like Nueva York."

"But does it have calles that would interest a king?"

"Yes, your majesty. It has all the calles in the world."

THE LITTLE NOVIA

23

SHE WAS a prisoner in the penthouse. She couldn't shop alone, go to the movies alone, or run her bath without seeing a cop behind the glass door. Someone named Dancer wanted her dead. And the cops wouldn't explain why. They were very civilized. They had walkie-talkies that could only tune into classical music.

"Is that Mozart?" she asked one of the special cops.

"Ma'am, I have no idea. It's a frequency protector, that's all. It keeps our radio band from flopping all over the place."

But the same policeman brought her one small miracle. Benjamin appeared out of the blue, wearing his leather coat, looking like a policeman. And she wondered if they'd recruited her little boy. He wasn't so little. He'd grown in the months since she'd been gone. And she couldn't seem to stop crying.

"Mama will never leave you," she said, "mama will never leave you." And she cursed herself for having tried to fool with Chase Manhattan Bank and the Christian Commandos.

"Does this Dancer want him too?" she asked the policeman.

"Yes, ma'am."

"Then I will take out his eyes and slap his pelotas and tear off his arms like the cheapest doll."

"That won't be necessary, ma'am. We have things under control."

But she'd frightened Benjamin with her outburst. They were both crying now. And he looked at his mama as if she were a wild animal.

She wanted to rock him in her arms, but the boy resisted her.

"Mama, I'm too big."

"I know, I know."

And she was like a wild animal. Half crazed, because she couldn't understand the course of events around her.

"Where's Professor Sparks?"

"Can't say, ma'am. We don't work for him," said the head policeman. "We work for the president of the United States."

She went to her phone, got the operator in Washington, D.C., and called the White House collect. The White House accepted the charges, which stunned the D.C. operator, who'd placed the call and was convinced that Yolanda Ramirez was one more crank.

"I have a message for the president from his little novia," Yolanda said. "He can give me letters of introduction and all that. But he'd better do a little explaining. I want to see Professor Sparks."

And she must have been a bruja, like Rafaela had said. Because her telephone rang in half an hour. It was Sparks.

"Explain yourself, Professor, or I'll scream and scream until the whole world starts to break."

"It's a simple story, Miz Yolanda. The courts unfroze Benjamin."

"He doesn't look like a boy who's been unfroze. He can hardly remember who his mama is. I don't blame him. Why are these policemen here?"

"Taita's ex-partner, Dancer Magallon, is on the rampage. And he'd like to hurt whoever's around Don Ruben."

"A cousin who kisses you every twenty years isn't exactly kin."

"The Dancer might not see it that way . . . don't worry. I'll clear up this mess."

And the professor was gone.

Then she heard a knock on her door, and she could feel some crazy static in the air, static that had come all the way from the White House. And there he was, Ruben in his purple pants, the dreamboat who'd been neglecting her. He was carrying blood roses, and the thorns bit into his hand. Yolanda understood. Blood red was his courting color.

"Ruben, have you come to marry me?"

"Yes."

And she fell on him, her little fists cracking his head back, and the policemen wanted to separate her from Ruben, but Ruben said no. His mouth was full of blood.

"Aren't you going to introduce me to your boy?"

Benjamin was hiding behind a chair and he wouldn't come out. Ruben dismissed the cops.

"I'll handle this."

He wouldn't wipe the blood. He had to crawl on his knees and appeal to the little boy.

"It's all right."

"You're bloody," Benjamin said from his vantage point behind the chair.

Ruben touched his face with a silk handkerchief. "There, it's better now."

And Benjamin ran into his arms.

"See, little sister, we get along famously."

"I'm not your sister. And put my son down. You fooled him with your smile, like you fooled me."

Ruben sat Benjamin in his mother's chair. "Don't go away." And then he turned to Yolanda, whose green eyes burrowed into him.

"You didn't get this apartment for me and the little king, did you, Mr. Falcone?"

"No. It was a neighborhood crib. Loisaida was one of our clearing houses."

"For cocaine."

"Sí."

"And all that fancy talk about missing Yolanda. Taita, you didn't have one damn thought about me."

"That's not true," Ruben said, clutching his roses.

"I was the little novia with her letter from the United States . . . the cousin who was left behind in El Norte, one more part of 'Operation Rescue Ruben.' You sang romantic songs about a Yolanda no one had ever heard about, and the Christian Commandos took the bait. Did I leave out a couple of points?"

"No. You argue like a general. But I did get you out of jail. And perhaps I was hoping that the Commandos couldn't convince you so fast, that you wouldn't be the perfect little novia."

"Jesus you expect an awful lot from a girl. Are all your mujeres on such good behavior?"

"Some," he said. "Some not."

"I guess I failed you, Don Ruben. Why the hell are you here?"

"To get you to be my mujer and marry me."

She was going to sock him again, but it was useless to hit a man who was scratching himself to pieces with blood roses in his hand. And so she turned coy around Taita.

"You haven't kissed me yet."

He held her in one arm and took half her head into his mouth. She'd never been kissed like that, not by her bank robber boyfriends or the jíbaros from junior high, those slicks with purple pants, like Don Ruben. They couldn't get her legs to shiver. And none of them knew how to swallow a girl's face.

That didn't mean she would marry Ruben. She had a child to consider. She was a mama again, and she shouldn't have been kissing any old man in front of Benjamin. He already had a confusion of fathers.

And so she pushed Ruben away, gentlelike. And she looked into his eyes. She had a long habit of falling in love with liars and bandits and bank robbers. And then Yolanda realized that *she* was clutching the roses now. That faker had put all them thorns into her hand.

BABYLON

24

THEY LEFT New York in a small caravan, Ruben, the little king, Yolanda, Benjamin, *and* Professor Sparks. The president wouldn't release Ruben without having a Commando in Bogotá, and Sparks had been elected to come along. Ruben didn't like it. But he had to accept a babysitter. Yolanda wore a blue dress. An army chaplain married them on the plane. Benjamin clutched his mama's wedding ring. Sparks opened a bottle of champagne.

"Compliments of the White House," he said.

Yolanda didn't know whether to laugh or cry. She told herself how happy she was and fell into a sadness that no champagne could cure.

Bailen met them on the runway reserved for him at El Dorado Airport. He was wearing his ceremonial sash. His soldiers were carrying assault rifles. There had been talk of another assassination attempt. The last two presidents had been assassinated, one outside the presidential palace, the other on his own runway at El Dorado. The guerrillas and traficantes were everywhere. They could seize an airport or a palace whenever they wished.

Bailen was fifty-three. He could have retired to Paris or Rome, where his books were adored. But he decided to remain in this hijueputa of a country where presidents did not survive their terms of office. Bailen looked like a lion. He had a stamp devoted to his image long before he was president. His writer friends thought the presidency was a big mistake. The South American Faulkner, they said, was asleep in the presidential palace. Where was the sequel to *La caeda?* Que putería! That was important. Not a man in a sash who was beholden to generals and had to live behind a glass shield. But they were unfair to Bailen. He wasn't searching to be another Bolivar. But he wanted his country to arrive at the end of that ultimate civil war he wrote about in his books.

He had television cameras behind him and could not waste a gesture. He planted a medal on Ruben's chest and installed him as his acting environmental minister. He kissed Ruben's bride, shook hands with that seven-year-old assassin, the little king, and posed with Sparks, the Christian Commando.

"With Don Ruben," he told the cameras, "we will create an environmental policy that has a cougar's teeth."

Then he boarded a bulletproof bus with the whole party, including the television cameras, sat very close to Don Ruben, one arm around his new minister, and encouraged him to speak.

The minister was shrewd. He didn't have his purple pants today. He wore blue serge.

"I'm only Bailen's little fist. I am at the president's disposal."

There were no crowds that Yolanda could see on the autopista, just a couple of stragglers along the route of the bus. They held the Colombian flag—children, mujeres, old men. How could Yolanda have known that Bailen had paid them out of his last royalty check to occupy that no-man's-land between El Dorado and the presidential palace and gawk at a bulletproof bus?

When he was only an author, Bailen could have gone anywhere, and he did. He had carne asada in the mountains with rebel priests. No one would have dared kidnap him. Yes, the traficantes had given him little gifts during those hard years between his novels. Yes, he had been some kind of bagman for Don Ruben. Druglords had slept in his house. But Bailen had murdered nobody. And he'd never been a thief.

Now the same rebel priests who could recite half of *La caeda* wanted to cut his heart out. And the Bailen who could once walk into any restaurant, who was welcome at any table, had to eat his meals with soldiers beside him. His wife, Marina, was on constant holiday in the Côte d'Azur. His boys and girls were at school in Switzerland, Germany, and France. He did not want them near continual death threats. And so Bailen was homeless, without a hearth. He lived in a palace that was bombed every six months, like some clockwork the traficantes had inspired.

And now he was riding in a bus with the man who had caused most of the chaos. Ruben had arranged those bombs, not to kill Bailen, but to show him that he could be killed. It was always cat and mouse with this maestro of the traficantes. Perhaps Ruben was the real novelista.

Yolanda could not see much of Babylon. The bus was heavily screened. It had huge metal eyelids above every window. But there was a skyline in the distance, enormous rose-colored monoliths that couldn't move her the way Medellín's Little Manhattan had done. Yolanda was a very loyal girl. She sat with Benjamin, who'd pulled the wedding ring off her finger and was wearing it now as some sign of his own "marriage."

And then the bus arrived at a building behind a big square and all the passengers were shooed into Bailen's palace like so many sheep, with soldiers of the Securidad forming a bridge on both sides of them and blocking Yolanda's view. She stood on her toe and glanced at a pigeon sitting on top of a flag.

There were checkpoints on every floor inside the palace. An armed guard sat in the cloakroom. Yolanda found a pistol in the women's toilet. Special bloodhounds sniffed for bombs. The dogs left hair on the carpets, and Benjamin had a sneezing fit. Yolanda hadn't even known that her son was allergic to dogs. Bailen saw her distress, and he had a gallada of maids vacuum all the carpets.

"My youngest daughter also had the rheum, Madame Yolanda. It cannot be helped. The dogs do very little. But the servants are at ease with dogs around."

And it was with Bailen's little act of kindness that Yolanda grew to like the palace. The mirrors were beautiful. The chairs were covered with gold paint. Some of them had been lent to Bailen from the French palace at Versailles.

The apartment she shared with Ruben was a suite of seven rooms, with a whole other galería for Benjamin and the little king. She could look beyond her bedroom and see a forest of doors that belonged to the same apartment. She was Madame Yolanda, the minister's wife. The maids wouldn't allow her to wash her own stockings in one of the bathroom sinks. She couldn't tell if she was a prisoner or a princess. Perhaps it was the same thing, as Bailen had told her at the party he gave for Ruben on the night after they all arrived.

"Please do not do your own washing, Madame Yolanda. It offends the maids, makes them feel futile. And we will have very bad morale at the palace. I cannot afford to be more of a prisoner that I already am."

Bailen was not a very good dancer, but he did the tango with Yolanda in honor of his new minister, a Medellín man. Bailen was too short and too slow, and Bogotá wasn't tango country. The musicians could not sustain that relentless beat of the tango medellín.

The new minister hid his fury. No one could induce him to dance. Neither Bailen nor his own wife. One of the generals came up to Taita and whispered in his ear.

"Always the fool, eh? Our presidente."

It was Muzo, wearing all the medals of his office, his face like a midnight mask under Bailen's chandeliers.

"Someone should ask the Storyteller to resign."

"I disagree," Ruben said. "The Storyteller holds the threads of the country together as much as he can."

"You didn't always think so, Don Ruben ... didn't you offer me millions of deutsche marks last year to kill the man?"

"Wound him," Ruben said. "Not kill. And the Dancer made that offer, not me . . . why didn't you take it?"

"Because I made more deutsche marks on my own with Bailen in power. But times have changed."

"Muzo, I'm here to help the Storyteller, not to drown him."

"Pity," Muzo said. "Think I'll cut in on Bailen and dance with your bride . . . someone has to help the Storyteller, eh?"

Muzo's tango had no more melodic line than Bailen's. He looked twice as foolish, because he tried to adopt the contemptuous mien of the tango dancer, and on Muzo it was only one more mask. He was like a doll in Yolanda's arms. But the medellínos didn't dare laugh. Muzo wasn't Bailen. Muzo would chop you off at the neck at the first sign of ambiguity toward him. He tolerated Ruben, because Ruben had been a traficante.

The dancing stopped. The musicians withdrew. Soldiers shut the ballroom doors. No one could get in or out. Bailen and his guests raised their goblets of wine and toasted the new minister.

"Skoal," said the Storyteller. "To Ruben Falcone."

"To Ruben Falcone," answered everyone except Ruben himself.

The clinking of goblets echoed off the chandeliers.

And then Ruben and the Storyteller disappeared. They'd gone behind the curtain that led to a private closet the Storyteller sometimes used as his study. But it couldn't have been so private. People in the heart of the ballroom could hear the Storyteller shout.

"I won't have it!"

A vein beat in the middle of Bailen's head like a silvery blue fork.

"Calm yourself, Excellency. You'll have stroke."

"Don't patronize me. I know what you're thinking. 'Little Bailen sits in the presidential seat, so Ruben can rule the palace.'"

"I have thought no such thing," Ruben said. "I want to help, Bailen. I want to help."

"Help? I had to take you, chinga. I cannot survive without American money. The president is not a bad man. His own wife visited the rain forests. She has contributed to the Colombian Red Cross. But how can I find stability if Don Ruben is one of my ministers?"

"I want to help."

"Shut up! I may have worked for you once, I may have lived off your coca dollars, like the rest of the country, but you do not own me, Don Ruben."

"I never did. I admired your work, so I let you have a taste of what I had. Your novels made me cry."

"Shut up. I will give you no authority, Don Ruben. You will be a minister without the slightest portfolio. You will have no say. You will talk to no other ministers. I will keep you locked in my palace. And if you defy me, Ruben, I will have you killed."

"Ah, it won't be the first execution," Ruben said.

"Shut up."

25

THE MINISTER had nothing to do. So he took Yolanda and Benjamin and the little king to a bullfight at the Plaza de Toros de Santamaria. The toreros were ridiculous in their pink capes. They all wore girdles to hide their winter fat. One of them, Domingo, had a wooden leg. He was the bravest, because he inhabited that invisible country between the toro and himself. Even with his awkwardness, he took risks. He held his line like a tango king when he killed. But he still disgraced himself. The toro he "delivered" had nanas and paper horns.

Ruben sat in a private box high above the bullring. He couldn't mix with the population. He arrived after everyone else, with a knot of soldiers, like one more enemy of the people.

He learned to sit at home in the palace. He made love to Yolanda, clutching her arms in that dank air, but he could not fall into the dream of his own embrace. Taita was preoccupied. Colombia was unraveling day by day, and Bailen could do nothing about it. Bailen raced to the Amazon when miners destroyed a campesino settlement that got in the way of their gold. He had to raise the price of milk and meat again. He couldn't subsidize certain staples and keep his government afloat. Bailen economized as much as he could. He moved into one large room at the presidential palace. He drank soup with the kitchen maids. He loaned the government money from advances on books he would never write. He grew a beard. He hocked half the treasures that had been given to him by friendly governments. He had his engraver, Alan Pizarro, who also lived at the palace, print more banknotes, but Pizarro offered to print dollars instead. Or deutsche marks. Bailen might have dreamt such a thing in one of his books. But this counterfeit currency would only have created a run on deutsche marks and dollar bills.

Bailen closed the doors between himself and the rest of the palace. He was almost tempted to start a novel. Ruben found him lying under a mattress, examining Pizarro's plates for a five-dollar bill. His eyes were raw from the lack of light.

"Go on, Bailen. Live like a peasant. Economize. But I'm a minister. I'll keep my seven rooms."

He seized the plates out of Bailen's hands.

"Give me back my money," the Storyteller said.

"No."

"I'll call my guards. They'll shoot you down like a dog."

"You have enough dogs at the palace, old man."

"I'm not old. I only look old. You cannot be president and also have your sanity. I keep getting gray hairs."

"Let me help, goddamnit."

"Hijueputa, what can you do? We have a million chinos de la calle. A third of our children have never seen the inside of a school . . . if I could educate those children, we might have a little bit of a future, no? The children are our last resource."

"Let me try," Ruben said.

Bailen stared at Ruben with his raw red eyes. He could have been a prophet or a renegade priest. He did not have the air of a president, or a president's clean shirt.

"What can you do? You encourage them to misbehave. You set a bad example. They all want to be traficantes like Don Ruben or Dancer Magallon."

"Let me try," Ruben said, and returned Bailen's counterfeit plates.

The little king was furious. "I'm not going to school. Why do you think I became a chino de la calle? I could have run to the priests. They would have adopted me, pappy. But I swore that I would never put on new clothes and study the alphabet. The alphabet stinks."

"You're going to school, like it or not."

Rudolfo took a razor out of his sleeve.

"Cut me, little man," Ruben said. "I won't resist." And he looked at Rudolfo with such disappointment that the little king almost cried.

He wore the clothes Taita had prepared for him. He brushed his teeth and combed his hair.

"Are you sending me to the school behind the palace?"

"No," Ruben said. "That's for the ricos."

"But I live here. I'm almost your adopted son."

"You're a murderer."

"So are you."

"I killed when I had to. That was my business."

"I also had my business when I was king of the calles."

"But this is Bogotá. And they don't like royalty from another town."

Ruben was only taunting Rudolfo, who was the most famous chino in the whole world of chinos de la calle.

They boarded a bulletproof bus together with a badolera of television cameras, rode to the southern outskirts of Babylon, and parked at a shantytown called the Villa Victoria, which was a neighborhood of dusty brown barns and little paper palaces on a hill.

The schoolhouse had twenty chairs and three hundred children. There was no blackboard and no books.

"Pappy, I think I'm going to fall in love with your school."

Rudolfo took his place among the three hundred children, who were electrified the moment he appeared. "The little king," they muttered, "the little king." Taita meant nothing to them. He was only one more minister. But they'd already heard legends about the gallada Rudolfo once had.

The cameras absorbed the entire scene: Rudolfo, the other children, the school, and the teacher, a law student who had volunteered to work in the Villa Victoria.

When it was Rudolfo's turn to spell his name, he said, "I can't."

"Then give me your initials."

"I can't."

And the cameras recorded that remarkable look of defiance and fear on Rudolfo's face, self-absorbed and haunted, like the country itself. That face appeared on the evening news. And no one could say how it happened, but chinos de la calle began showing up at schools in all the barrios of Colombia. These children didn't own television sets; perhaps there'd been some rumor that the little king had surrendered himself to Bogotá's school system.

Bailen wasn't content at all.

"You tricked me, Ruben. You volunteered that little assassin, and the schools will be flooded with assassins like him."

Ruben seized the Storyteller by his filthy shirt.

"They are children, señor."

"Yes," Bailen said. "You're right. But my minister of education does not want you to interfere."

"Your minister of education is a hijueputa. Bailen, I need a small army."

"What?"

"Lend me your environmental rangers."

"Impossible. They belong to the Department of Agriculture."

"Bailen, they belong to me."

"I can't. My ministers are already jealous . . . it will create a rivalry."

"Your ministers have their assholes tucked under the ground. Go on, print your paper money, but I have to borrow your rangers."

"For how long?"

"As long as it takes, señor."

The rangers were housed in an old stable behind the Plaza de Toros. Their entire residence smelled of horse and cow dung. The inventory of rangers had dwindled to ninety men. They were laughed at by every other constable in the country. They carried Colt Commanders, but they were loathe to use them. They could be fined severely if they ever shot at a man, but the rangers had become everybody's target. Gold miners and children and mad old women shot at them and sometimes killed a ranger.

They were lying around in blankets when Ruben visited their stable. He had a document with Bailen's signature. Their leader, Leonel Escobar, the novelista, perused the document before he said hello.

"Minister, I am under your command, but the morale is lousy. We are shot at everywhere we go."

"Why so formal with me, Leonel? Didn't we drink rum together in Bailen's house? Didn't we chase after the same women? And Leonel, you usually won. I was only a billionaire. How could I compete with a poet?"

"Taita, that was a hundred lives ago."

"I will be your sponge, Leonel. I will take the bullets in my own chest."

"They wouldn't shoot Taita."

"Then work with me. I need your men."

"That time in the Amazon, when the professor had his dynamite, and all the miners surrounded us, it was only a bluff, wasn't it, Taita?"

"Sí."

"The professor rehearsed it like a symphony. He realized Taita would rescue him and the rangers."

"Sí. It was his way of introducing himself. And now, Leonel, we have to find Professor Sparks. He's a gringo, and I do not want him to suffer alone. The Casa Blanca has asked him to watch over me. But I will have to babysit for the babysitter."

"Yes. That's how things are done in Bogotá."

And Leonel woke up all his troops.

Sparks had never really lived at the palace. He was a Commando and he didn't like four-poster beds and maids who laughed at the fur on his chest. And so he moved into a cheap hotel, far from the Plaza de Bolivar, where a five-dollar bill could get him a bottle of Ron Medellín and enough company for a week. He meant to go to the A.A. meetings at the gringo church on the Carrera Septima, but somehow he couldn't get there in time. He suffered blackouts, but so what? It was better than writing reports on Don Ruben for the president of the United States. Sparks was a field man, not a fucking nanny.

And so he lapsed into a solitude where a perico or a puta's tit were his only consolation. He drank himself blind, then sucked on little cups of coffee and placed calls to Q Street that never got through. And then, coming out of a bender, he watched a bunch of bandidos in black headbands pick him up and toss him in the shower. Rusty water rained on him.

"I'm not an infant," he cried.

"Yes, you are."

"Who's that? Who's that?"

"The minister for environmental affairs."

"*And* his rangers." Sparks started to laugh. "Ruben, you're a goddamn genius. You pulled them away from Agriculture, didn't you? And now I can go back to the States."

"I want my babysitter. Not to babysit, but to walk point for the rangers." Ruben lied a little. He didn't want to abandon the professor to a bottle of rum. The Casa Blanca would never release him while Ruben was a minister.

"What's your program, little father?"

"To kick ass," Ruben said. "And to revive the Greens."

"I'm ready," the professor said, swallowing some Ron Medellín.

26

THEY WERE like shock soldiers in Ruben's hands. They'd venture into alleys, meet with the fiercest galladas. No one shot at them now. Ruben promised amnesty to all the pirates who offered to go to school. "Like Rudolfo," he said.

And he found no resistance, not even in the remotest favella. He rescued bands of starving girls from the policemen who would have placed them in child prostitution houses. And he raided all the child houses he could find. He didn't have a Colombian poncho or purple pants. He wore ministerial blue. He arrested no one, because he didn't have the power to arrest. He was a civilian, and the rangers weren't real cops. But he kicked the child houses to pieces. And though he never once fired a gun, ministers started to complain. Don Ruben, they said, was stealing their mandate. He had no authority over prostitutes or government schools. He didn't even have a ministry behind him. All he had were his Gestapo troops.

Bailen recalled him to his palace.

"You are unsettling the government, Minister Falcone. My generals are itchy and the ministers are threatening to resign."

"Let them resign," Ruben said.

"And if my government should fall?"

"I'll build you a new one . . . Storyteller, they complain because I'm getting results. I can't save all the children, but I can save some . . . I'm going to Medellín tomorrow with my rangers."

"Agriculture wants them back."

"Tell Agriculture that the rangers are on permanent loan to me."

"You must not ask them to kill."

"They aren't policemen, Bailen. They're not allowed to kill . . . adíos."

❧

But he could not find one authentic gallada in the barrios of Medellín. Just a few starving cripples and dogs. Someone had pulled the children. He went to Securidad headquarters on Junin Street and asked for Colonel Jacob, who was still under house arrest. Ruben had to present his minister's papers before a corporal would lead him to the colonel's little room. All the braids had been torn from Jacob's tunic. His beard looked blue in the dingy light.

"Colonel, where are the chinos de la calle?"

"Muzo has them, but I'm not sure where. This isn't Bogotá, Don Ruben, where at least Bailen has the illusion of power. His name means nothing in Medellín. He's a scribbler, that's all."

"You don't have to tell me that. I'm a paisa, like you."

"Then walk away before you are killed."

"You threatening me, Isadoro?"

The colonel laughed inside his empty tunic. "How could I threaten? With what?"

"Then help me," Ruben said. "Isadoro, for once we're on the same side."

"Rumbeaderos," the deposed colonel said. "I think Muzo is hiding them in the rumbeaderos of Medellín . . . the rumbeaderos are now his cattle cars."

"But these cattle cars cannot move."

"Be careful, Taita. Muzo wants your life."

"Hombre, should I get you out of here? I could sound my own alarm."

"No," the colonel said. "I'll sit."

And Taita marched to the Rumbeadero de la Paz with his men. There were thousands of children inside, packed like inmates of a concentration camp. The children's eyes seemed to glaze when they saw Taita, as if he'd walked into their own hallucination.

"Hombre," Ruben said to the captain sitting near the door. "You owe me some chinos de la calle. Several thousand, I think."

The captain grinned. "Minister, take them from us, why don't you?"

"The children might get hurt."

"Then in my opinion, Minister, you are standing in a pile of shit."

"Not at all, hermano. I just planted a bomb under your little table."

"Liar," he said and looked under the table, where a tiny box began to tick.

"You wouldn't dare," he said, shivering. "You wouldn't dare."

"Why not? Hermano, let's all die together, no?"

"You were always crazy," said the captain, "even when I ran drugs for you and the Dancer."

He signalled to his soldiers and abandoned the rumbeadero to Don Ruben. It took hours to feed the children, but the news had spread. Rangers were wiring up all the rumbeaderos, according to the Securidad. Ruben freed sixty thousand children. But he was running out of cash, and he couldn't draw on his foreign accounts in time to feed the children and transport them to Bogotá, which wasn't so hostile to the Republic.

He visited the Medellín office of the Banco del Panama. He sat down with the bankers, who were reluctant to involve themselves in the Republic's internal affairs. But Ruben was eloquent in his ministerial colors. "Gentlemen, I am asking for a private loan. I don't have to explain my backing. Call Basel. But if you don't cooperate, the bombs might go off, and I cannot be responsible for the anarchy that will follow. There will be lootings, señores. Money will be lost."

The bankers had to choose between Muzo and this minister. They authorized a loan of three hundred thousand dollars, and Ruben was able to rent all the trucks that were required to transport the chinos de la calle.

Ruben sat inside the Rumbeadero de la Paz, which was empty now. He was all alone. The rumbeaderos had always been the traficantes' central marketplace, even during the years of Guillermo Gaudí. That was the reason they'd never been bombed . . . until Muzo went against all the secret treaties and bombed the Rumbeadero de la Paz, hoping to get rid of Ruben.

He had a Coca Cola and dark cigarettes brought from the cafetería across the street. Ruben was waiting, but waiting for what? Perhaps the remembrance of old times at the Paz, when he danced and traded perica for a pocketful of emeralds.

And in came the Dancer while Ruben sat and dreamt with his dark cigarettes. The Dancer was also alone. He didn't have his squad of assassins. His purple pants were dusty. He took off his dark glasses and sat down next to Taita without kissing him.

"Why did you come back? To join this bobada of a government? Hermano, I gave you a honeymoon for life . . . I reached into my own pockets so that Taita would have an uninterrupted cash flow."

"And a very quick burial. Eduardo, you sent assassins after me and my family."

"Because you have a soft heart for this Republic. That is fatal in our business . . . please, my throat is burning. May I have some of your Coca?"

He drank from Taita's bottle and began to sob like some inconsolable infant.

"Stop crying into the Coca. I don't want to drink your tears."

"But I'll have to kill you the next time I see you. It makes me sad."

"It's only your imagination," Ruben said. "You've been planning to kill me for years. That's one of the reasons I left. Your greed was appalling. But I couldn't bring myself to kill you. You're my oldest friend . . . except for Yolanda."

"She's only a woman, Taita."

"And my novia."

"That's why she doesn't count. I love my wife. I love my children. But I never made blood vows with them . . . Taita, I miss you, and you aren't even dead. Every minute you're in Medellín you shame me."

"Should I order another Coca for us? You've slobbered on my bottle."

"I have to meet with my captains and plan your death."

"*Our* captains," Ruben said. "I still own one tenth of the cartel."

"Goodbye," the Dancer said. But he didn't move. He sat and sat over Taita's bottle of blackened sugar water. And then he walked out of the Rumbeadero de la Paz.

27

BAILEN WAS alarmed by the army of chinos de la calle that arrived in transport trucks. The capital was already choked with children. But *El Tiempo* was suddenly lionizing him for this children's crusade. "Has El Presidente woken out of his long sleep?" And like some extraordinary somnambulist, Bailen put on a clean shirt. His barber shaved behind his ears. He wore a suit that he'd bought on the Rue Tournon in Paris, during his years as a literary lion.

The maids slapped the dust out of his mattress. They opened Bailen's shutters. He had to blink. He folded a silk handkerchief into the display pocket of his suit like a flower with polka dots. A sentence twirled inside his head.

"We, the weary matadors of lust and love . . ."

He wondered if it was the itch of a new novel.

He went with his elite guard into the brown streets of Bogotá. People recognized him. "Pappy, pappy, teach our children," they said.

They kissed his hand, and it felt like the luna de miel of his first weeks as president, when flowers arrived from all over the world and people looked at him as their Buddha from the Caribbean . . . until he had to raise the price of bread.

The little king was in all the headlines. Taita too. And they were part of Bailen's administration, no? Perhaps the only part that mattered. His other ministers had failed him. But he couldn't oust his acting minister of justice. Muzo owned the air force. The navy was a scant armada that had to patrol Colombia's Atlantic and Pacific coasts, and seemed loyal to no one but itself. And the army, Bailen's army, had been flirting with a military takeover ever since the Greens had come into power. And so the Storyteller had to tiptoe.

Congress couldn't do very much. The Capitolio Nacional had been bombed more often than the presidential palace. Senators were shot down in front of their doors. Others were kidnapped and found dying, with black bags over their heads. So Bailen and his ministers ruled mostly by decree. He seemed to be coming out of his hibernation.

"Los Verdes," women shouted from the windows. "The Greens, the Greens." Thank God he didn't have to meet with his finance minister and talk about ration stamps and yet another ceiling on government spending. He would spend, spend on the schools. Because without these children the whole Republic would die. He had no other mandate. He didn't care if snipers shot at him from the rooftops. Rebel priests could write slogans against him on the walls of Bogotá. He was Bailen, only Bailen, the Storyteller and president of his people.

The owners of coffee bars on Calle Ocho begged him to stop for a drink. And Bailen had a tinto every five or six blocks. His figure could be seen for half a mile, Bailen bending over a coffee cup, muttering, "Como esta, amigo?"

He walked south into the barrios populares. Even his own guardsmen were a little afraid.

"Bailen," their comandante said, "it is not wise to provoke the poor with your presence. They are hungry, and they will see us in our uniforms and you with your silk handkerchief that cost a month's wages. They are socialists and even worse. They sympathize with the guerrillas. They will ask for our blood."

"Comandante," Bailen said, "it was the barrios populares that elected me, not the northern suburbs."

"Sí. But now they will vote with their claws."

"I do not believe it," Bailen said. And he was right. He'd never been a novelist of the upper classes. If he'd hurt the poor with his "shock program" of price increases, it was to save a government that was close to ruin. He'd had to sacrifice his own Green policies. Our Green fascist, the rebel priests had called him. But Bailen was no fascist. He was a president in an impossible time.

Campesinos kissed his hand. The poorest grocer offered him a piece of fruit. He bit into the fruit and raised his fist to acknowledge his support of the barrios populares. He traveled further south, into the favellas, the shantytowns that had no running water or electricity, just paper shacks on a hill. He entered the schoolhouse of the Villa Victoria, where the little king was learning how to write his name and had become the most celebrated schoolboy in Bailen's Republic.

The school had gained another hundred children with Taita's "trucklift." The students had simply extended the back wall of the school another fifty feet. Their professor was sick today. A few members of the Securidad had knocked him on the head for teaching "socialism" to a gang of mestizo brats. The professor had told a television crew that the price of oranges was too high, and now he had to pay his own price.

And Bailen was here this afternoon as a substitute teacher. He wasn't grandstanding, puffing out his reputation as a peddler of words. He'd stumbled into a teacherless class and started to teach. He banished all the television cameras.

"Señoras y señores, this is not a circus. I have a class to control."

He walked among the students, looking at their pathetic notebooks, which were filled with an unintelligible scrawl. They could not count. They could not spell. They were analfabetos.

"Chinas y chinos, today we will have a lesson on the letra *B*. Consider in your head all the words that begin with the letra *B*. Recite the most famous ones."

"*Bailen,*" said a very eager boy.

And Bailen held out his arms like some maestro of children's music and said, "*Bailen, sí.*"

"*Bogotá.*"

"Sí, sí."

"*Bahia.*"

"Sí."

"*Boca.*"

"Sí."

"*Babilonia,*" said the little king.

And Bailen was almost suspicious. "Sí."

"*Benjamin.*"

"Sí."

"*Bella.*"

"Sí."

And Bailen challenged every child, drawing words out of them and shaping the words with his fluttering hands, so that *Boca* looked like a cavern, and *Babilonia* was an over-turned hill.

The reporters watched Bailen outside the barren windows of the school. They had never seen such animation from this man. The cameras captured him inventing a vocabulary for the Villa Victoria. And Bailen, who'd been waiting for a fall inside the presidential palace, who'd been the caretaker of his own doom, was now mastermind of the children's crusade.

"Hermanos," said one of the cameramen, who was amazed by Bailen's ability to conjure with his hands. "All the generals and war colleges in the world will not defeat this man. I think Bailen will fuck the fuckers. What do you think?"

He now had a family again. Yolanda, Benjamin, and the little king. Madame Yolanda was more like a widow than a minister's wife. Because Ruben was chasing grievances all over the Republic as the new porte-parole and executioner of the Green Party. There would have been no Green Party without Ruben. And Bailen would brook no complaint about Ruben's encroaching on the territories of certain ministers. "The rangers are his." And he wouldn't rein in Don Ruben. But that made his environmental minister even less of a husband. He was never home at the palace.

Bailen began having dinners again. And Yolanda became mistress of the palace. She welcomed foreign heads of state, this convict girl. She would dance only once or twice with the same minister or king. She had that intense, overpowering look of a woman waiting for a man.

Bailen would venture abroad with her, into the bowels of the city, where they would watch a cockfight or eat a simple meal at some panadería and stuff themselves with cake. It disconcerted Bailen that his doubles were appearing all over town. He'd never had doubles before, not even after his success with *La caeda* or the mad days of his election. He was becoming an icon, like Guillermo Gaudí, the president who would leave his palace to instruct the poorest children in the ways of the alphabet.

He was no longer the captive of his generals and economic advisors. He'd become a dangerous man. His admirals decided not to ignore him. Senators sought his advice. He did need his engraver, Alan Pizarro, because the Republic could not float along without a "hit" of paper money that Bailen himself used to buy deutsche marks, so that his schools could tolerate more and more chinos de la calle.

He was often photographed with the little king. It wasn't for exposure. Bailen wouldn't have traded on the popularity of a boy. But they looked good together, Bailen and Rudolfo.

"Bailen, where's my pappy?"

"Fighting the fascistas."

"Will he come home?"

"Soon, soon. He doesn't even give his schedule to a president. But he's smart. This way, no one can surprise him."

"When can I become a ranger?" the little boy asked.

"When you learn the alphabet, hijo de puta."

But Bailen was sorry. He shouldn't have called the boy a little bastard. They were all like widows without Don Ruben.

INDIOS

28

HE'D WALK out of bombed buildings, nursing a scratch under his eye. The Dancer's assassins had come after him. But they were always a little too slow. Muzo's commandos de la muerte were also after his life. But he was the tango king. And he could dodge bullets like no other dancer. He wasn't indestructible. He would bleed after a battle. But no one knew how to make him die.

The Dancer's assassins were all cinephiles.

"Did you see *Lawrence of Arabia*, hijueputa?"

"You mean the pelicula about the gringo who fights on the side of the Arabs?"

"Sí."

"I saw it twenty times. It was the longest pelicula in history."

"Que putería! Who cares? But the gringo is like Taita."

"Taita doesn't have yellow hair."

"Hey, brujo, I'm not interested in your yellow hair. Taita is Lawrence of the Amazon. I personally shot him in the ass.

I nicked his ear. But it means nothing. He can heal the worst sucking wound."

"He's a mago, like the men in Bailen's book."

"No, he's a traficante who has betrayed us."

And they continued to shoot at Ruben, sometimes drawing blood out of the phantom. But they could not kill him. And the Dancer grew morose. He could not bear this inexactitude of Taita neither dead nor alive. He was secretly glad the asesinos had failed. But it was cutting into his image as the new druglord of Medellín and king of the traficantes.

He had a conference with General Muzo, more an enemy than a friend. He despised Muzo and loved Don Ruben.

"General, I am losing face. I finance your commandos de la muerte, but they cannot bring me the minister's corpse."

"They wound him, and nothing happens. But why blame me? Your assassins have had no more success."

"What troubles me, señor, is that they are all ex-commandos. Perhaps we should hire men from outside the country."

"Don Eduardo, that will look very bad. The foreigners will think they we cannot settle our own accounts."

"But at least we will have a corpse."

"What if they fail? We will look doubly foolish . . . no, it is better to stick to the ones we have."

"And where is Taita now?"

"In the Amazon. With his rangers."

"Attacking the gold miners? We will have a very bad image, señor, if our miners cannot collect the gold. The foreigners will think of us as crazy people. Miners being molested by civilian soldiers."

"The miners are armed, Don Eduardo, and Taita is not. It won't be a contest for very long."

"Ah, but you have not lived with Taita, General, or worked with him. He will destroy all their El Dorados. Wait and see."

But Ruben would walk into a mining camp, two pistols tucked inside his belt and a hand grenade pinned to the vest of his blue serge suit, which he wore in the jungle as a sign of his ministry. The miners remembered him as a ruthless traficante. And when they saw Taita at the head of the rangers, with Leonel the novelist and that alcoholic gringo, Sparks, they weren't so sure of themselves, even with all their mujeres and mercenaries.

Ruben was never impolite. "Señores, I have a deposition from the government. I would like to see your sales slips for the liquid mercury."

"Begging your pardon, Minister, but what business is that of your government?"

"Have you not seen Bailen's new decree? Liquid mercury that has been bought without a government stamp is now considered contraband."

"Minister, we will gladly get the stamp."

"Bailen will not issue it to gold miners."

"Then we are at an impasse."

"Sí."

They stared at the pistols and the hand grenade, and had the image of Taita wading in their precious water without boots, like some angel of death. They were deeply religious men. And so they picked up their camp, with the water pumps and the putas, and moved a couple of klicks upstream.

Again Taita would appear. He was no longer polite. He

dropped his hand grenade into a water pump. The pump would explode and bleed chunks of metal into the river. They would have to kill this crazy minister from Bogotá. But only the mujeres would shoot at him, and the mujeres would always miss.

Ruben had destroyed their dream of El Dorado, and they quit the Colombian Amazon. But there were always more miners, and more encounters with the minister in the blue suit.

It ended in a stalemate, with Taita and his rangers neither advancing nor retreating, but they saw fewer cases of mercury fever. The settlements above and below the camps weren't so vulnerable to the ravages of El Dorado.

But it was the rain forest, with a rhythm of its own that could swallow miners and mujeres and environmental cops. Taita was distraught. Because he hadn't seen one birdman in all his forages. The Indios were gone. A few old men sold beads and blowguns at some settlement near Benjamín Constant. One or two women had been turned into putas. Taita bought them back from the settlement, but these women had nowhere to go.

"Where are your tribes, mamzelles? Where are my birdmen?"

The women had no answers for Taita and no home. He tacked them onto the rangers, warning his men not to sleep with these women who belonged to the Indios. But the women were offended, thinking Taita had told the rangers they were diseased. They flirted with everyone in Taita's band. He had to let them sleep with his rangers or the women would have become terribly morose. And of course they were business people and had to be paid. In deutsche marks. And so Taita had simply exchanged camps for these women, who were now putas in his own employ. The bird-men would never forgive them.

He foraged deeper into the forest. Campesinos joined his band. Stragglers from everywhere attached themselves to Taita. He had a thousand camp followers and an army of two hundred men. Soon there were so many followers, that Taita's army lost the element of surprise. They could not raid a camp of gold miners. But the miners also grew frightened of so many faces behind the trees. And they would desert their camps the moment they could hear the crackle of men and women in the forest.

And then Taita's army fell upon another army. The anti-drug police, with their escorts from El Norte, officers of the Drug Enforcement Agency, who still considered Ruben a druglord and wanted to search his camp.

"Nice to meet you in the wilderness, son," said Larry Shavers, tactical advisor to the whole antidrug war. "I've been hearing stories that the rangers are nothing but mules, that you're carrying for the Dancer. We've been smoking out his fincas, but we can't find any product."

"Too bad," Taita said.

"We have more firepower, son. Best to cooperate with us. Because you're going to stand for a search."

Taita took Shavers and banged his head against a tree.

"I'm a minister of this Republic, and if you interfere with my mission, I'll have Bailen toss you out of Colombia."

"Bailen don't mean shit," said Shavers, wiping his head with a handkerchief. "I work for the president of the United States."

"So do I," said Professor Sparks, rocking his shoulders

between Don Ruben and the DEA. "I'm Sparks of the Christian Commandos."

"I know who you are," Shavers said. "A goddamn renegade who runs around with druglords and their pimps."

"Well, why don't you get the White House on the horn and see what's what?"

"Funny boy," Shavers said. "I'd look ridiculous, sending out signals from the middle of the jungle. You'll stand that search. And I'm going to arrest Don Ruben. I have the power."

But the antidrug police were reluctant to seize a traficante who was also a minister of state. Governments were fickle affairs. Taita might move to Finance one day and freeze all their salaries. So their captain whispered in Shavers' ear. Shavers turned red. His eyes darted with a kind of madness. Then he regained his irony and bowed to Don Ruben.

"You win. No search."

Sparks was recalled to the United States. El Presidente needed him for another mission. He hugged Ruben.

"I'll miss you, hombre. Say goodbye to Yolandie for me . . . and watch out for all the goddamn gold miners."

But Sparks shouldn't have worried. Taita's aura seemed endless in the rain forest. The rangers didn't have to fire into that thick jungle air. No one resisted Taita. He still couldn't find his birdmen. He suffered as his army swelled with other Indian women who wore the cheap red paint of Western civilization. Taita laughed a bitter laugh, because the Colombian traficantes were known as "Indians" in the

United States. And the Indians seemed to have disappeared off the face of the forest.

People left him little gifts. The putas offered to sleep with him without their usual compensation.

"I have a mujer in Bogotá," he said.

He hadn't written Yolanda or phoned her since he'd entered the jungle. Taita lived as if he had no history behind him. He'd become a creature of the forest. He plucked at the huge lilies in the water that looked like gigantic toadstools. He bathed his wounds. Leonel himself acted as Taita's surgeon. He'd gone to medical school before he was a novelist. And he would run after Ruben with a needle and attend to all the sutures.

Taita felt like he was on some crusade with no Saladin in sight. He was fighting enemies that no longer made themselves visible to him or his army. Finally someone did appear in the form of a rebel priest. Padre Enrique, commander in chief of the Dividing Hand, the most formidable guerrilla group in Colombia, composed of peasants and priests. Enrique was a maoist in a world where there was almost no memory of Mao. He'd also been Ruben's teacher once upon a time, at a Catholic school in the barrios of Medellín. He'd caned the boy, pulled on his nose, but had also given him startling lessons in economics. Ruben had learned all about Robin Hood from Enrique.

And now, coming out of the bush in combat boots, he didn't smile at any of the rangers. He was scornful of the women's bare breasts. He carried a rifle rather than a rod for whipping bad boys. He put the rifle down and attacked Taita, socking him mercilessly while the rangers looked on. But Taita would allow no one to interfere. He took the punches and the slaps. Old wounds began to bleed. Sutures unraveled. Ruben blinked.

"You've joined that fraud and his government," Enrique said. He was a little man. He barely reached Ruben's shoulders. But the whole country feared him. He levied taxes on the traficantes and distributed that tax money to the poorest farmers. Ruben couldn't have prospered as a traficante without Enrique, who controlled the Amazon as much as any man could control it. Enrique believed that the revolution would come to Colombia. But Taita knew that it was only one more fable of an ex–Catholic school teacher and priest. The Dividing Hand couldn't stop that crazy spiraling of stock markets all over the world, a world of consumer goods and not revolutionary pamphlets. Enrique was a relic who had incredibly powerful teeth. The army couldn't destroy him. He collected his taxes and declared Bailen's government null and void. Enrique had his own republic in the rain forest and foothills. He taught peasants how to read and bombed government palaces. Senators stayed home because of Enrique. The judiciary was at a standstill. But Enrique wouldn't have his revolution no matter what he did.

"You're Bailen's lapdog, Don Ruben."

"And if I am," Ruben said, the blood forming giant blots under his shirt. "I still have a program."

"What program? You ungrateful shit! I taught you how to dream. You'd never have become a billionaire without me."

"And who tithed every deutsche mark I ever got?"

"I have my own church, Don Ruben. Now tell me about your program."

"I will push the miners out. I will educate the children. I won't hurt the rain forest."

"Ah, the magnificent Green Party," Enrique said, and socked Ruben all over again. "But will the campesinos really breathe all the oxygen you and Bailen give them?"

"Yes . . . help me, Padre."

"I will kill you first. You deserted the Indios. And now they are living in a terrible gloom."

"You know where my birdmen are?"

"I've been feeding them, you bogotano shit."

"Please, Padre . . . take me to the Indios."

"Why? So they can build you another Finca Dolores with their own backs?"

"No. If they're gloomy, I will talk to them. I don't want the Indios to die."

"And you won't enlist them in your latest madness?"

"I promise."

❧

And so Enrique led Ruben and his ranger army into the guerrilla stronghold, a kind of jungle fort at the neck of a river that had never been mapped. The journey took three days. Crocodiles snapped at Taita and sniffed his blood. Enrique cracked them on the head with his rifle butt. And when Taita saw his birdmen, he started to cry.

They'd become grandfathers in the months Taita had been gone. Their hair was lusterless. Their bellies had enlarged. They would eat nothing but a special mush that had no nourishment at all. But when they saw Taita's wounds, they livened a little. They boiled different pieces of bark, put them into a compress, pissed on it, and applied each compress to Taita's wounds. The wounds healed. Taita smoked black cigarettes with his birdmen.

Watching the birdmen prosper all of a sudden, Enrique said to Taita, "Go on, you little dog, take them with you."

"Padre, I could . . ."

"Don't talk money, or I'll cut your throat."

"And you'll declare a moratorium for nine months . . . you'll promise not to bomb Bailen."

"Why on earth would I do an idiotic thing like that? Muzo is paying me a fortune to bomb."

"But Muzo will only be one more dictator."

"I can deal with dictators. I understand the logic of their minds."

"Padre, he'll pay you and then he'll hunt you down."

"It's of no importance. I'll hunt the hunters."

And now it was Taita who fell on Enrique, grabbing his cheeks and giving a terrible twist until the padre was almost blue. Enrique didn't scream for help. The guerrillas had known Taita since he was a boy.

"Padre, start your revolution, but I want a chance."

He let go of the padre, who coughed once and recovered.

"Tell the maestro that his fiction has gone to the dogs. Bailen can't even write sentences anymore."

"He's president of the Republic. He doesn't have to write."

Taita left that stronghold of the Dividing Hand, with his birdmen, the rangers, and the putas who covered their breasts in the company of these Indios and turned chaste. Taita's army grew. He policed the rivers. The miners stopped bringing mercury into their camps. They carried sacks of gold and sediment out of the jungle.

No one ridiculed the rangers anymore. The antidrug patrols kept out of Taita's way. He'd slept in the White House, after all. And when he was in Bogotá, he lived with Bailen, inside the presidential palace.

29

SHE KEPT hearing about his exploits. Taita the Miracle Man. He was developing a grand army of Greens around him. The generals were reluctant to mention Taita. The admirals concerned themselves with foreign fishing boats in Colombian waters. Muzo agitated against him at the Ministry of Justice and inside his own air force. "The man's a civilian. He has no right to raise an army." He tried to have Taita killed, of course. But he couldn't succeed, and so he started rumors of Taita's ambition. "Hombres, we have to prepare ourselves against a coup. This Robin Hood has the Indios on his side."

"Los Indios," the senators said. They wore pistols to prepare themselves for Taita's raid on the capital. They locked their wives in the country somewhere.

"Los Indios."

"That's ridiculous," Bailen said. "He's freeing our rivers of mercury rot. The rangers have harmed no one. And I'm not worried about los Indios."

He'd meet Yolanda in the palace during lunch. It hurt him to see her sad eyes. All the dispatches he'd sent into the jungle couldn't bring a response from Taita. But Bailen had never been more beloved in the barrios populares, which didn't share the senators' obsessions.

"The lad's an ingrate, Madame Yolanda. He keeps all of us in the dark. But he is serving his country . . . and the Green cause."

Yolanda said nothing. She couldn't really miss such a ghost. And for her Ruben was a ghost, like Guillermo Gaudí. Ghost husband, ghost lover, and little ghost cousin out of her past. She wasn't even sure why she was still in Bogotá. Was it loyalty to the ghost or fondness for El Presidente, who had no real friends at the palace other than Yolanda or Benjamin and that wild boy who'd suddenly become a scholar. Rudolfo, the little king.

She returned to her suite. Benjamin was at school. She heard a soft, rhythmic clatter in one of the seven rooms. Yolanda thought it was the maid. But a maid wouldn't have moved like a tango king. Taita had returned from the Amazon. He wore pistols in his belt. His lips were pale. He smiled. "Que tal?"

"I know who I am," Yolanda said. "Tulipa Dawn."

Taita sat down. "I'm tired."

He was beautiful in his chair, with the light off the shutters landing on his face. She had to use all her concentration as a Christian Commando in order not to kiss him.

"I'm Tulipa Dawn."

"My body hurts, and you welcome me with riddles."

"I'm Tulipa Dawn and you're my tango king who dances with me once or twice . . . and goes away."

"You're not Tulipa," he said, his temples beating in that profound light.

"Why did you marry me? Was it because a minister needed a wife? And you said to yourself, 'Why not Yolanda?' "

"I love you and I didn't want to bring a puta into this house."

"You love me so much that you wander everywhere in order not to love me."

"That's my nature."

"I'm Tulipa Dawn."

"You sit in the dark," Taita said, "and your imagination grows."

"What else do I have? I wait for you."

"You have your son."

"Sí. Thanks to you, I'm a mother again. But I'm your woman, Ruben, like it or not."

"I have bad habits," he said. "I cannot be constant all the time. And Bogotá can never be my home. I'm a paisa."

"And I'm one more piece of furniture in a picture palace."

"That is unkind . . . I missed you."

"Sí. You sent me letters twice a day, phoned me every hour . . ."

Taita gritted his teeth. "I was in the Amazon."

"You're a clever man. You could have improvised, Don Ruben."

"I'm your husband. Please don't call me Don Ruben. My enemies call me that."

228

Yolanda curtsied to that hombre in the chair. "You're my very own lord, I suppose. Minister Falcone."

He started to shiver. And half of Yolanda's anger was gone. She undressed him, saw his wounds, welts that looked like hard flowers burrowing into his flesh. She walked him to their marriage bed, where she'd been mostly a virgin, imagining herself as Tulipa Dawn.

She placed him onto the bed, and she couldn't stop looking at his lips. His hand reached for hers, and suddenly they were kissing. Where had all his passion come from?

"Taita, you'll hurt yourself."

"Mujer," he said. "Keep quiet. You're not Tulipa Dawn."

The town seemed to demand a parade. Taita's picture was chalked on every available wall, sometimes with Bailen, sometimes not. He was the undeclared minister of the Amazon. He'd fought the mining interests. He'd met with Padre Enrique and the Dividing Hand. The rebel priests were giving Bailen's government a little honeymoon. And so there was this crazy caesura in the civil war, a certain *drôle de guerre* that was neither an armistice nor a genuine offer of peace from Enrique's guerrilla government. But Bailen had time to breathe. The barrios populares and the ricos of the northern districts began to see Bailen and his new minister as their saviors. Don Ruben had journeyed into the Amazon, had suffered terrible wounds. He was the magician of Bailen's book, the caballero who could not be killed.

The Greens prospered.

The antidrug police stopped burning acres of forest to force the traficantes out of their fincas. The death squads had quieted down.

Generals began to court Don Ruben. Admirals too. Even if his blood turned to water, they argued, he could be the next president. They also demanded a parade.

Taita wouldn't ride in a bulletproof bus.

"That's madness," Bailen said. "Do you remember what happened to El Presidente Kennedy?"

"Bailen, we don't live in Dallas . . . and how can we arrive in the barrios populares like shivering rats?"

"Then I must have my guardsmen on the running boards . . . and I must select the route. The Avenida Caracas has too many buildings like the Texas Book Depository. It would be an open invitation for someone to slaughter us."

"Select the route," Taita said. "But I don't want your guardsmen breathing on me."

Bailen had his custom-made Lincoln brought out of the palace garage. And while he waited, that zambo, ChiChi, walked up to Taita and whispered in his ear. Taita nodded once and the zambo went away.

"What did he want?" Bailen asked. "I should have arrested that man long ago."

"It's nothing, Bailen. Get into the car, please."

And Bailen, wearing his medals and his sash, stepped into the Lincoln, where Yolanda, Benjamin, and Rudolfo had been installed. Yolanda wore a blue dress. Her hair was swept back. She looked like some elemental goddess who was married to that enigma, Don Ruben. His blue serge suit had corroded on him in the Amazon. He wore a white winter jacket in the Bogotá spring. He held Yolanda's hand.

Benjamin had seen so little of him, that he couldn't figure out this daddy who wasn't a dad.

The little king was poised on the jumpseat. The car left the palace. Bogotanos waved at him and the whole presidential family. They had to peek between the shoulders of Bailen's guardsmen, who carried machine guns inside their coats.

The Lincoln crossed Calle Ocho.

"Bailen," Taita said, "I think we should let Enrique police the Amazon. He might do a better job."

"He already polices the Amazon . . . to fatten his pocketbook."

"And feed the campesinos."

"Must we argue?" Bailen said. "Enrique has his government. I have mine. Mine may be an illusion, but it is the only illusion I have . . . where's General Muzo?"

"In his own palace."

"He should be here with us."

"Bailen, do you want him to ride on the running boards with your guardsmen?"

"I'd feel safer," Bailen said.

"So would I . . . excuse me for a moment."

Taita climbed out of the car, kissed a couple of children, and was gone, leaving Bailen to pout. He did not want to sit without Taita. It wasn't a proper parade. People danced close to the car, trying to touch Bailen's hand, but the guardsmen wouldn't let them near El Presidente.

He felt isolated, even with the presidential family. What a woman this Yolanda was, with ankles Bailen himself might have adored. How did Taita have the will to leave her so often? He had a terrible fit of gloom. He wanted to rush out of the Lincoln and hide in his own little house of words. But he couldn't build such a house anymore. He'd forgotten how to scribble.

He heard a kind of panic coming from the streets.

"Los Indio, los Indios."

He had to shove two of his guardsmen away, so that he could peer out at all those faces. And then he saw what the commotion was about. Taita's birdmen had come to Bogotá. They wore business suits, but their eyes and mouths and cheeks were painted blue and red. And they flitted among the bogatanos in bare feet. Like wizards, they ran and disappeared.

Taita returned to the presidential motorcade at the corner of Carrero Dice and the Avenida Jimenez. His white jacket was a little soiled. His right eye was swollen. He clutched Yolanda's hand, smiled at the little king, and sat Benjamin down on his lap.

But Bailen wasn't completely satisfied. "You should have told me about the birdmen, Taita. Someone might have been harmed."

"Someone like you or Yolanda and me."

"Ah, it was Muzo again. He scheduled a bomb for us, eh?"

"Sí."

"And your birdmen defused the bomb."

"Sí."

"I think it's time we had another acting minister of justice. Who would you recommend?"

"Colonel Jacob of the Medellín Securidad."

"Isadoro despises you."

"He's still the strongest candidate. And he's not a thief.

But how will you depose Muzo? The man has his own air force."

"I'll reflect on it."

And Bailen sank into the cushions in his ceremonial sash. He was the president, after all. In the middle of a parade.

30

BAILEN GATHERED all the admirals and generals he could around him. His popularity was growing even as the Colombian peso went down and down. He was the new strongman of Bogotá, and chancellor of the Greens. There were no bread lines. Oranges could be found in the streets. The chinos de la calle were flocking to school. And Colombia had become more than cocaine. So Bailen went with his admirals and his generals to Muzo's private palace on Carrera Dice. General Muzo didn't function out of the Palacio de Justicia, which had become a ruined shell after the Dividing Hand had seized it in '92 and held it for six days. Muzo had decided on a floating ministry, which could be dismantled at will, like the Finca Dolores. But he lived at the palace on Carrera Dice. And he didn't fortify himself against Bailen with soldiers from the Securidad.

He met Bailen in his living room, while the admirals and generals waited in the hall.

"Ah, Bailen," he said with a long mestizo smile. "You've been dreaming to put me under house arrest."

"Not at all. You can have your air force. But you must step down as minister of justice."

"And if I refuse?"

"Then I will go on the television and ask the people to choose between you and me."

"That's clever, Bailen. And I will bow to your wishes. But please understand. You have an enemy for life. And not even *La caeda* will save you."

"Perhaps. But I never relied on the reputation of my novels."

"Still, I'm curious. Who will be the next minister?"

"Colonel Isadoro."

"Ah, the little paisa. I believe he's sitting in jail at the Medellín Securidad."

"No," Bailen said. "I've released him."

"Excellent. But do me the kindness, Bailen. Take your jackals and get the hell out."

"Of course, General. I wouldn't want to intrude."

And Bailen walked out of the palace with his tail of admirals and generals. Muzo's soldiers trembled a little. They must have realized that their fate was with the novelista now.

Bailen grinned like a mountain burro. It was almost as good as rediscovering all the sentences he had lost. But he didn't grin very long. The Dancer had left an invitation for Don Ruben at the presidential palace.

Taita,

Oblige an old friend. Meet me at the Rumbeadero de la Paz in Medellín Monday next. Nine at night. And without Bailen's men. Do I have your word of honor?

—Dancer Magallon

Bailen was horrified. "I'll have Colonel Jacob surround the rumbeadero. We'll kill him."

"No."

"Taita, it's a trap."

"We were partners, Bailen. I have to go."

"Are you such a fool that you will give our victory away? He's counting on your paisa stubbornness. He knows . . . this is Muzo's work, I promise you. Sweet revenge.

"You're from Cartagena. You don't understand our ways."

"Then go. And what will happen to the Greens? You and the Dancer will kill one another, and Muzo will inherit it all. The miners will sing at your funeral. The forests will be plucked. The terrible inflation will come again. And we will have nothing, nothing . . ."

Taita excused himself and started to pack. The little king clung to him.

"Take me, pappy."

"I can't. You have to go to school."

"I'll skip school for one day. I'm a fast learner. I can write my initials now."

"Ah, if I let you near Medellín, you'll run back into the streets."

"But then you'd have the chinos de la calle on your side."

"We don't want chinos de la calle. We want school children."

"Pappy, I would come without your permission, but they won't let me on a plane. I'm too small."

"Hermanito, go to school."

He hugged the little king. He had no idea what would happen in Medellín. He could never see the lines of his own history. He packed. The little king went off with his school

236

books. Taita looked in the mirror and saw Yolanda's face. It startled him. His own reflection could have been transformed. Her eyes seemed haunted in all that glass. She was a little taller than Taita, and he felt as if her shadow had enveloped him. Tulipa Dawn.

He kissed her. And he could have been dancing. Because there was a sway in her hips. She didn't scold him or chide him or beg him not to go.

"I'll be back," he said. "Tomorrow."

She wasn't frozen. She didn't start to cry. They continued their little dance.

He left for El Dorado airport. And that's when Yolanda collapsed into herself like a pumpkin. She could hear her own body howl. She was mourning that tango king of hers. She took little Benjamin into her arms. The boy was petrified.

"Mama, you're hurting me."

And Yolanda could feel herself come out of that crazy pumpkin.

"I wouldn't hurt my little chick."

And for a moment she stopped dreaming of the Rumbeadero de la Paz where Guillermo Gaudí had discovered the tango medellín.

❧

All of Latin America had come down to one thing. El Dorado. The thirst for gold. It didn't matter if that gold was in the form of emeralds or cocaine or bananas or rubber trees or little nuggets in the Rio Amacayacu. The conquistadors had dreamt of El Dorado and gave birth to a whole shuddering continent, a lost land of gold. But Taita wanted to

climb out of that dream. He'd become his own conquista-
dor, a narcotraficante who distributed "white gold." It was
one more El Dorado, a dream search into some mythical
place. But he no longer needed the myth. He wanted the
forest to multiply and the rivers to run without mercury
vapor. Only the Greens could break that grip of El Dorado
on Taita's sad continent.

And so he'd gone to meet the Dancer in Medellín, not to
rob him of his white gold, but talk to him mano a mano.
Taita was no idiot. He knew the Dancer meant to kill him in
the rumbeadero. So he brought his birdmen along. They sat
on the flight to Medellín in their business suits, their faces
painted some neutral color. They had no ammunition other
than their blowguns and their darts, which they carried in
the billfold pockets of their suits. Ah, Taita thought, El
Dorado had been turned on its own head. These primitive,
wondrous men had had their own dream of gold long before
the conquistadors.

Other passengers stared at them.

Taita smiled.

He took a taxi from Jose Maria Cordoba airport with his
Indios into the heart of Medellín. The taxi driver shivered
behind the wheel. The sun fell from a sky that turned its
own color of pollution pink. They stopped at a café near the
rumbeadero. Taita drank a tinto. The birdmen all had Coca
Cola Grandes. They sucked at the big bottles with a moun-
tain of teeth.

People began to enter the Rumbeadero de la Paz. Taita
could hear the orchestra. It was only in Medellín that there
was a proper beat for a tango dancer. Heartless, and very
slow. "Hermanos," he said to the birdmen, who received no

Spanish at all into their vocabulary. They read Taita's eyes and abandoned their giant Cokes.

They didn't go into the rumbeadero with Taita, because they would have scared the entire population of dancers. They stood next to the door. Their shadows were enough. And Taita entered the Paz. It was exactly nine o'clock. Dancer Magallon was in the middle of the floor. He had his porkpie hat and purple pants. He wore the dark glasses of a Blues Brother and a traficante. He had his assassins all around him, his own *commandos de la muerte*.

The orchestra stopped playing.

Dancer Magallon clapped his hands. "Hombres."

The orchestra started up again, while the Dancer tapped its beat with the crush of his heel. And the tango artists, who could have been Taita's double, danced with their own ladies of the night.

Taita and the Dancer kissed.

"Hermano, you shouldn't have brought your Indios. I asked for a friendly visit."

"Then why did you bring your assassins?"

"Taita, look, they're about to shit their pants."

"But why are they here?"

"To kill you. I'm always planning to kill you. But you're the only brother I have. It isn't so much fun being a billionaire."

"You could retire."

"I'd be shot dead in five minutes and some bogotano would replace me . . . I'm your buffer, Taita. I keep you alive."

"And help Muzo plant a bomb in front of my motorcade."

"It was a trifle. I wasn't serious. I paid the zambo blood

money to warn you in time. And I defused every other bomb with my own hands. But I will have to kill you. It is necessary right now. Muzo will not lend me his planes while you are alive. I'm losing millions. I can't transport all my shit."

"Then why don't you kill me instead of writing me a letter?"

"I sweated over each word. I'm analfabeto. I had to hire a professor from the university to put in all the punctuation. I am frightened of periods and commas."

"Eduardo, you did well. Tell me what it is we have to discuss."

"Your death. I would like it to be a glorious one."

"I'm glad, but my birdmen wouldn't let you leave here alive."

"I'm not worried. I will cover my neck. Their darts will have no bite. My brujos will find antidotes to all the poisons they carry."

"Then take out your knife, Eduardo. I am sick of this little game. I breathe only because you cannot bring yourself to kill me. I'd rather not breathe at all."

The Dancer revealed his knife, which he'd held in his palm like a boy's secret candy. But he didn't even have the opportunity to raise his arm. He was shot five times in the back and crumpled up into Taita's arms, like some lonely tango dancer.

"Puta de madre," Taita said. The other tango dancers *and* their women were all carrying Colts. Taita understood their disguise. They were members of the Securidad. Colonel Jacob himself jumped out of a dancer's costume, while his officers arrested all the commandos de la muerte.

"You didn't have to kill him," Taita said.

"He was holding a knife."

"You didn't have to kill him."

Taita stooped and placed Dancer Magallon on the floor. "Cover him up. He'll get cold."

"I'm going to arrest Muzo," the colonel said.

"And after that you'll kill me like your grandfather killed Guillermo Gaudí."

"I'm not my grandfather. And you're Bailen's minister."

"But I'll become a danger to whatever order you decide upon . . . you didn't have to kill him."

"I'm a Green, like you, Don Ruben. And I'm in your debt."

"And it's because you are in my debt that you'll have me killed."

"No."

"Sí. You're a paisa, colonel. But I cannot kiss you. You murdered my friend."

Taita walked out of the rumbeadero. His birdmen followed behind him. They weren't wearing shoes.

ABOUT THE AUTHOR

A Guggenheim Fellow, Jerome Charyn has taught at Stanford, Rice, and Princeton, and is currently teaching film history at the American University of Paris. *Death of a Tango King* is his twenty-eighth novel.